LOVERS
IN ARMS

by
Osiris Brackhaus

LOVERS IN ARMS

© 2019 by Beryll & Osiris Brackhaus, Kassel, Germany
All rights reserved. No part of this work may be used or reproduced in any manner whatsoever without permission from the author, except as allowed by fair use. For further information, please contact osiris@brackhaus.com

Disclaimer: This is a work of fiction. It contains explicit violent content and is intended for mature readers. Do not take the events in this story as proof of plausibility, legality or safety of actions described. Even though this story deals with real, historic events, the story and all characters therein are purely fictitious. Real, historic personalities appearing are not meant to be accurate representations, but adapted characters for the dramatic purposes of this fictitious universe. Also, while great care has been taken to be as accurate as possible in many details regarding the period has, some details were deliberately changed to fit the story. Please don't assume you could pass a history test on this novel alone.

Second Edition
Proof: Julia Weisenberger
ISBN-13: 9781077003910
First Edition
Editor: Rylan Hunter
Cover Design: D.M Atkins and Siolnatine
Cover art: Natalya Nesterova

www.brackhaus.com

Dedication

To my lovely wife.

Blurb

U.S. Army Captain Frank Hawthorne returns to Germany, against orders, to testify at the Nuremberg trials. He's attempting to save the life of Johann von Biehn, a former Nazi Officer. No one at the trials knows that three years ago, at the height of the war, Frank had been sent to kill the very man he is now defending — and that Johann is the love of his life. Frank must not reveal what happened between them during the war, but that leaves Frank with hardly any evidence to counter Johann's notorious career as a Nazi.

Contents

Chapter 1 - Jump into the Fray................................9
Chapter 2 - My Crazy German............................19
Chapter 3 - Getting Closer....................................33
Chapter 4 - Spying for Beginners........................51
Chapter 5 - Connecting the Dots.........................65
Chapter 6 - Coupling..79
Chapter 7 - The Morning After............................95
Chapter 8 - A Brush with Disaster....................105
Chapter 9 - Thunderstorm..................................117
Chapter 10 - Desperate Measures.....................129
Chapter 11 - The Lovers......................................143
Chapter 12 - Of Friends and Farewells............161
Chapter 13 - No Dead Heroes............................173
Chapter 14 - Some Things Never Change.......185
Chapter 15 - Epilogue - Bellagio.......................199

Chapter 1
Jump into the Fray

September 1946, Nuremberg, Germany

One of the hardest things Frank ever had to do in his life was to step out of the train that had brought him to Nuremberg.

He had jumped out of planes, accepted covert black ops, killed people simply because he had been ordered to. Yet nothing had ever demanded so much courage, such foolhardiness of him as what he was here to do this time.

In the end, it was another passenger — eager to get out of the train — who basically pushed him onto the platform. With far less drama than Frank had anticipated, he set foot on German ground again.

The pale gray morning light didn't do anything to hide the scars the war had left. Walls were still pockmarked with the traces of gunfights, and the beautiful train station's west wing was nothing but a neat pile of rubble. Beyond the station, the silhouette of a castle loomed in the early morning haze, somber and latently aggressive. It was the Nuremberg castle, namesake to the town he was in to do his business. Here the world held court, judging over the fates of the remaining heads of Germany's Nazi regime. And Frank was called to serve as a witness in one of those twenty-five trials.

But, unlike the other times he had visited this country, this once, Frank was not here to kill. He wasn't here because he had been ordered to, on the contrary.

This time, he was in Germany to save the man he loved.

***

September 1946, Nuremberg, Palace of Justice, Room 600
"I do not think I have to point out the sincerity of this trial to anyone. Captain Hawthorne, do you swear to speak only truth, and nothing but the truth?" Lord Judge Lawrence asked sternly, and behind him, Frank could hear the soft murmur of the translators in the background.

"Yes, I swear." Again, in the whisper of the translation, Frank could hear his own words repeated in many languages. As he spoke several of them fluently, it felt like an eerie echo that added to the already sufficiently oppressive scene, like ghosts of the past narrating his words to those who couldn't listen any longer.

"Prosecution, your witness."

Frank blinked in irritation. It was unusual for the prosecutor to be the first to question a witness of the defense. But then, there was hardly any precedence to be found for this occasion. To his left, Chief Prosecutor Robert H. Jackson made a great show of sorting through his papers, giving Frank the unpleasant opportunity to take in the details of the place.

The whole room, more a large hall than anything else, was crammed with people. He was facing four judges, four prosecutors, all of them with their respective aides, representing the victorious Allied and Soviet forces.

At the rear of the room, a whole battalion of reporters from all over the world, legal advisers, historians, all sorts of civilians. Translators, a dozen of them, were turning his words into any language needed almost the moment he spoke them. Thick bundles of cables were running from the microphones on their desks all through the room, feeding their words to the headphones of everyone who needed their assistance.

To his right, caged in by heavily armed Allied troops, a single German Nazi officer and his lawyer were sitting. Graf Johann von Biehn, Oberst of the Wehrmacht, was still looking the way Frank remembered him — tall and lean, his dark blond hair neatly parted, his gray uniform suiting him so perfectly as if having been especially designed to look smart on him. A true-blooded Aryan if there ever was one. But Johann also looked tired, his aristocratic face almost as gray as his uniform, and he seemed lost on the huge, somber benches of dark polished wood that were so terribly over-abundant in this place.

That all the walls were covered with equally dark wooden panels didn't do one thing to lighten up the mood. It only made the white helmets of the guards stand out even more.

If only Johann weren't looking so terribly subdued, Frank thought with a sudden pain in his chest that almost made him flinch. *Why doesn't he even look at me?* It was so hard to reconcile the laughing, debonair and exhaustingly brilliant man in his memories with the prisoner he saw in front of him.

But then, Chief Prosecutor Jackson apparently decided that he didn't need any papers in this case and briskly walked over to the small stand in the middle of the central floor where Frank was waiting. He was a short man, but still his voice effortlessly filled the large room.

"Well, Captain Hawthorne. I hope you had a pleasant flight here." The smile that graced his square features didn't even once reach his small, cunning eyes.

"Yes, sir, thank you."

"Apparently, the attorney for the defense was convinced that you could add something helpful to his hopeless case."

"Objection!" a voice from the right exclaimed, and Frank could hardly suppress a smile. The last time he had seen the man who now acted as an attorney at law in one of the world's most prestigious trials, he had been sitting on the back of a cattle transport on a desperate flight out of Nazi Germany. That time, Elias had been an emaciated refugee, but even now in his impeccable suit, his voice hadn't lost one bit of its deceptively boyish, guileless clarity.

"Mr. Jackson, with all due respect to your personal opinion, shouldn't we leave the judgment of my case to the judges?"

Soft snickers in the background were all there was to be heard for a few heartbeats, then Lord Judge Lawrence said, "Objection accepted. Strike last comment from protocol."

It was obvious by Jackson's face that he thought it audacious for the defense to even exist, more so for daring to raise its voice. And he took the judge's unspoken rebuke as a personal affront.

"Of course," Jackson said, brushing back his thin, dark hair and taking great care to recreate a semblance of neutrality to his features before he went on. "Well, Captain Hawthorne, whatever circumstances enabled you to speak here as a witness for Oberst Graf von Biehn, your own government made pretty sure we know basically nothing about. Which, to be honest, doesn't really make you a suitable witness, in my eyes."

Whatever he had expected the witness to reply was not said; Frank didn't join him in his game. Instead, he stood there at ease, hands folded behind his back, waiting politely until he was asked a proper question. For a few seconds, the two men stared at each other, both trying to figure out what made the other so goddamn sure he was doing the right thing while obviously not doing so.

Frank could almost see himself reflected in Jackson's stare. With his freshly pressed uniform, broad shouldered and athletic, his dark brown hair in a neat crew cut, Frank probably looked every inch the perfect, all-American soldier to him. His angular face handsome in a plain, masculine way, his dark eyes looking serious and somewhat distrustful. A relatively new scar on his cheekbone added a roguish flair that even Frank found rather dashing.

Little wonder Jackson had a hard time figuring out what had made Frank end up on the apparently wrong side of the whole affair. He didn't look like a traitor. Or a pervert, for that matter.

"Captain Hawthorne. Would you consider yourself a patriotic person?" Jackson finally asked. "That is, would you ever do anything willingly that you know would harm your country?"

"No, sir, I wouldn't." Genuine scorn was simmering in Frank's voice as he added, "I consider myself a patriot, a soldier and a good Christian. And my military record will surely prove this beyond any doubt."

"I definitely do not doubt you in this case, Captain. Just for the record." Jackson smiled like a snake ready to strike. "Is it true that you had been living in Oberst von Biehn's manor for about two weeks in August 1943?"

"Yes, sir."

"Had he been working for the Allied forces?"

"No, sir."

"Were you there to start such collaboration?"

"That information is classified."

"Of course." Jackson took his time to scratch his head pensively before he went on. "Was there any indication at any time that Oberst von Biehn would consent to such collaboration?"

"No, sir."

"Is it also true that he was considered one of the finest military strategists of the German Wehrmacht?"

"Yes, sir."

"A close personal friend of Reichsminister Goebbels and several times recommended for his sly military and political maneuvering by Hitler himself?"

"Yes."

"A trusted and renowned member of the Nazi Elite?"

"Yes."

"And is it true, that after a few days in his presence, you aborted your mysterious mission?"

Silence spread in the large hall at the last question that had been as much of an accusation as anything else. Frantically, Frank was searching for an appropriate answer, but his prolonged silence was already giving away far too much.

"Please answer my question, Captain."

"I independently changed my mission objective, yes, sir. I got recommended for outstanding performance in the field afterwards."

"Of course." Jackson smiled as if Frank had just pointed a rifle at his own chest. "And what do you think, Mister Hawthorne, what are we to make out of your appearance here? Except that this man has not only been privy to all the military and humanitarian crimes of the Third Reich he stands trial for, but also had a vital part in conceiving them? And that his persuasive skills were dangerous enough to sway even your otherwise so patriotic mind?"

"Objection!" Elias' voice cut through the tension. "Witness is led to assumption."

With a cold feeling of dread, Frank wondered if coming here was actually helping Johann. Right now, it sure didn't look like it.

Compared to this, jumping out of planes over enemy territory was child's play.

***

August 1943, airspace above Lübbenau, Germany

Jumping out of planes at night over enemy territory becomes, if not exactly child's play, then at least pretty normal if only done often enough.

"Captain?" a voice from out of the dark somewhere close to the cockpit yelled through the small aircraft. "Are you ready? We're approaching Lübbenau."

Instead of trying to raise his voice above the noise of the plane's engines, Frank flashed a thumbs-up at the airman, readying his parachute. Swiftly, he had gone through the usual checks, his other equipment in another bag on his chest.

Strange how things like this can become routine, he thought to himself as he walked over to the gaping dark hole he was supposed to jump through. Darkness spread below him, above him, a shapeless mass of unrelieved black. Except, maybe, for the occasional tiny lights one could guess on the ground and the ominous, pale glow at the horizon.

He had seen on the maps that his latest assignment would lead him within fifty miles of Berlin, but that it would be this close Frank had never imagined. Below him, the Spreewald spread in the night, a large forest covering a unique part of the river Spree, which later would run through the very heart of the Third Reich.

Within this forest, Oberst Johann Graf von Biehn had his manor where he would host the largest meeting of military attachés in Germany since the beginning of the war. And it was Captain Frank Hawthorne's job to go down there, find that manor, then hide in the swamps and forest long enough to assassinate von Biehn and two of his guests. If, in case the rumors were true, Goebbels attended the auspicious occasion, he would become Frank's primary target.

Funny enough, surviving and returning home had not been among the explicit orders he had received.

There would be, like every time, certain arrangements to ensure he would be able to return. At least, theoretically that would be the case.

But Frank grinned at the thought that his last eight missions had never been rated better than "return probability zero." Standing here was the best proof that even the eggheads in HQ didn't know all. He had survived the Algerian desert, Siberia, Paris and several missions in Germany. Tonight would be the sixth time he would dive into the realm of the enemy to take out some of their indispensable Aryan masterminds.

Admittedly, this mission was more dangerous than any of those he had been on before. But then, every mission he took on seemed to be more dangerous than the one before. Worst thing that could happen was that he got killed. No great loss.

"Captain Hawthorne?" A face appeared out of the darkness of the plane's interior, framed by a massive headset. "We're about to reach drop zone. Last chance to decide otherwise."

Frank only laughed at the suggestion.

He had not risked the lives of this plane's crew to turn weak at the very last moment. No one could say how long the radar gap at the Baltic Sea would remain open, and they had to make use of any plane they got through unnoticed.

The young airman next to him nodded silently, his face clearly showing that he had not expected any other reaction. Also, he smiled at Frank with a certain patriotic admiration that made Frank want to slap the boy. Luckily, at that moment the airman turned serious, yelling, "We're there! Ready?"

Frank nodded, unhooking his safety line, and leaned out the open door.

With a slap on the captain's shoulder, the other man yelled, "God bless you, sir! Go!"

And Frank jumped.

Immediately, the infernal noise of the plane receded, replaced by the comparatively soft hiss of air swishing by. As they had been flying very low to get underneath the enemy radar, he instantly opened his parachute, cursing like he did every time at the violent jerk as the cloth suddenly slowed his fall.

But not as violently as usual.

Alarmed, Frank looked up; trying to figure out what was wrong, barely able to see anything above him in the darkness. There was something odd with his parachute's shape, and some of the lines looked tangled. Frantically, Frank pulled at the strings to maybe unfurl the cloth completely, but to no avail. The main part of the parachute was working, but not enough, and the asymmetry made it simply impossible to steer the blasted thing.

Now this would be a stupid way to die, Frank thought with a certain frustration. Below his feet, the forest came closer at an alarming speed, and there was no way he could have tried to find a place to land where he wouldn't get skewered by a branch. Helplessly, he watched himself hurtle down to the ground less like a stone but like a shot duck; for the first time in his life he was serious with his praying.

He crashed through the forest's roof, twigs and branches hitting him as if an entire football team was taking turns practicing their tackles. With an ugly, wet sound, he smashed into the muddy ground, his chest blossoming in pain, his legs feeling like they had been cut off.

"I must find a place to bury my parachute," Frank murmured aloud as he struggled to keep his consciousness, and rapidly lost the battle. "Damn me if I ruined my rifle..."

Chapter 2
My Crazy German

September 1946, Nuremberg

It was late at night when Frank left the court to walk back to the guesthouse he was staying in. Maybe he would be lucky and find a pub or a restaurant on the way that was still open at this hour. It would be nice to be in a German pub while not on a mission, for a change.

During the day, the soft mist that had been hanging in the air upon his arrival had condensed to a veritable curtain of clouds, and though it was still relatively warm, a soft drizzle was falling. Kicking at the puddles at his feet, Frank wondered if there was any way this day at court might have gone worse.

He had hoped to help Johann by coming here, not to offer this blasted prosecutor the perfect arguments. But then, there had been no other way of answering without outright lying. Johann had always made sure he kept an impeccable façade among the Nazi. Only now, exactly that might become his downfall.

But hiring Elias as his defending attorney had been a brilliant move of Johann's, Frank had to admit.

Before the war, Elias had been living in Potsdam, running his own small practice before he had been forced to close it. Jews had no longer been allowed to run businesses, and definitely not as a lawyer. Elias had been trying to get by for some time, tried to get his family out of the country, had gotten himself into trouble and then into the mercy of Oberst Johann Graf von Biehn; who had smuggled him out of Germany in a cattle transporter, together with his family, some other fugitives, and a pretty stunned American assassin.

Elias was an amazing person, and if it hadn't been for his occasional encouraging smile during the day, Frank would have seriously considered quitting the whole thing and leaving. Johann had simply been sitting there, listening to him, looking at him. But no small nod, no smile, not a single gesture of recognition, nothing that would have indicated that he still felt anything for Frank.

This insecurity was a torture more exquisite than any of us could have come up with, Frank thought with a grim smile. At least, he had managed to get permission to visit Johann in prison tomorrow.

Frank had been so sure, so unshakable in his conviction that there would still be something in Johann's heart for him, something that would maybe even match the love he still held after these three years. But the German officer sitting in court had so little in common with the dazzlingly charming man who had served him red wine and poetry late at night such a long time ago. The thought of maybe having risked so much for nothing made Frank feel suddenly nervous, groundless as if having jumped out of a plane without yet knowing if the pack on his back contained a parachute or merely a stash of laundry.

"Hey, you!"

The shout yanked Frank's moody mind back to the present, less because of the arrogant tone but more due to the fact that indeed the person had been yelling in English.

"I'm talking to you, are you deaf?"

With a certain mellow surprise, Frank watched as a group of five GI's approached him in the narrow side street he had been walking through. Their sand-colored uniforms looked far too crisp and dry to belong to a group of men out for a beer or two, and they looked far too sober and alert for that anyway.

Disconcertingly so.

Somewhere beyond, a car turned on the huge square in front of the main station, filling the small street for a second with painful brightness. Then it was gone again, leaving nothing behind but the soft sound of the drizzle and shadows that now looked even darker than before.

"What do you want?" Frank asked, his voice conveying far more fatigue than he had wanted it to.

"Nothing," the speaker of the group replied, stopping a few steps ahead of Frank. "Just wanted to ask you a couple of questions."

More and more, Frank's senses that had been dulled in a day of banal and almost depressing court proceedings came back to life, alert with the definite feeling of trouble brewing.

"Then ask. I'm tired."

These soldiers were all wearing their proper badges and colors, Frank noted. *So they think they've got nothing to hide.*

"You've been at the trial today." The speaker seemed angry, annoyed, and most of his men apparently agreed with him. "You've been trying to dodge Jackson's questions."

"No." Underneath the fatigue in Frank's voice there suddenly was a new emotion, and it took even himself a moment to notice it was raw anger; anger at having to defend himself, anger at being accused for doing the right thing, anger at his own people acting the superior race all of a sudden. "I have only been trying to stick with the truth."

"Stick it up your ass!" the young GI in front of Frank snorted, his body getting ready to strike.

The way he was nervously fingering his knuckles clearly showed that it was precisely what he actually wanted. "Who do you think you're helping with that?"

"Sorry?" Frank just didn't want to believe it. "I'm trying to help a friend. A good man who, if not entirely innocent, is not guilty of the crimes he's on trial for."

"He's a goddamn Kraut!" By now, the young soldier was almost yelling, and Frank scanned the alley for a quick route of escape. Unfortunately, there was none he could see at the moment. "What did he offer you? Money?"

"You're forgetting yourself, Sergeant." Still Frank tried to stay calm, but inside, he was fuming. *How did that boy dare!* "You have no idea what you are talking about."

"No, of course I don't. I only see how the people here lived in fear before we freed them, what they did to those wretches in the camps. I only know how they killed my brothers!" Slapping his chest to emphasize his last words, the GI looked like he was close to tears. "How can you stand there and call yourself an American! Don't you have any pride?"

"Stop it, boy!"

"How dare you! You bloody collaborators are even worse than that Nazi scum whose boots you're licking!"

Hurling himself at the young soldier in complete disregard of his friends and their firearms, Frank punched him square in the face, noticing his nose shattering with grim satisfaction.

From there on, everything else went very fast.

Mere moments later, all five GI's were down on the wet cobblestones, unconscious or cringing in pain. Their guns were lying safely out of reach, either on the other side of a wall in some backyard or well away down the gutter. They were decent fighters, but no match for a man trained to survive on his own when the odds against him were far worse.

"Listen to me, boy," Frank said as he knelt down by the first GI, handing him a handkerchief, almost feeling sorry for the bloody mess he had made of that young man's nose. Almost.

"Next time you want to get all patriotic, pick on someone your own size. Maybe one day you'll learn that not all Germans are monsters and not all Americans are heroes." Standing up, Frank straightened his soggy clothes. "As you have just proven."

Turning around wordlessly, he left the alley for the square in front of the station, not even looking back once.

Oddly enough, Frank noticed that this incident had done tremendous good for his mood. He felt angry, hungry, and definitely way better than before.

Time to find a pub and get some *Bier und Schnittchen*.

***

August 1943, Spreewald, Germany
Somewhere in the sluggish depths of Frank's unconscious mind, a simple thought sparked to life. For a timeless moment, the plain and simple feeling of pain was the only thing there was. But soon enough, its existence roused other emotions from their sleep.

Urgency was the next one to come back to life, followed on its metaphorical heels by duty, and fear.

Somehow, between the four of them, they actually managed to spark the first tiny bit of real consciousness, and immediately, Captain Hawthorne was wide-awake, a soundless gasp on his lips.

Bright sunlight, pale and yet vibrantly alive was the first thing he realized of his surroundings; falling through a small, segmented window to his right. Outside, some kind of ivy had to be growing, dark shadows of leaves moving within the patch of light.

Frank tried to move, but a searing bolt of pain from his chest and left leg told him he would be ill advised to do so. He clenched his teeth, closed his eyes, and tried to calm his heart that was still pounding with the shock of sudden pain.

Wind — wind in the trees outside — was the next thing that his half-awake mind recognized; soft and constant wind. A musty, slightly moldy scent was in the air, cool and unmoving.

Wherever he was, he had to be inside, and Frank didn't like the implications one bit. Blinking, he opened his eyes again, and this time concentrated on making more sense of the dark shapes he made out beyond the glaring light.

Slowly, the shapes around him turned into a large mechanical lawnmower, and for a heartbeat, Frank feared he had been hurt more seriously than he had thought. But the odd image remained, and one by one, more equally unexpected items joined.

A garden hose, rolled up and covered with cobwebs, a shelf with countless jars containing dried flowers and seed pods, spades, shovels and a manure fork. Two folded garden recliners, a large gypsum bust of Hitler, half covered under a pile of pillows, and a tin bucket filled with small swastika flags on sticks.

If it weren't completely mad, Frank thought, *I'd say I ended up in a Nazi garden shed. A pretty big Nazi garden shed.*

Moving only his head didn't prove too painful, and so he studied his surroundings more thoroughly. Frank noted with certain amazement that he was lying on another recliner, underneath an impressively ugly brown crochet plaid. Whoever had put him here had taken good care that he was all right.

Beneath the blanket, Frank was still wearing his pullover and trousers, but his jacket was gone, and most importantly, all of his other equipment as well.

But he was still alive, and that was the first step in getting all the other problems sorted out.

Underneath his pullover, Frank found that there was a thick bandage covering his chest, and his left foot was equally wrapped up. Why any German should do this was beyond Frank's grasp, but he didn't feel like complaining, either. Wouldn't be the first time he was lucky beyond belief.

When he hit the ground, he must have severely sprained or even broken his left foot, Frank assumed. Maybe also broken a rib or two; quite bad, but definitely not as bad as it could have been. And if the bones were not broken, he still had a realistic chance to fulfill his mission. If he got out of this shed in time.

At least it didn't look like a prison, and right now, that seemed like a good thing. It made it seem unlikely that whoever had put him here would interrogate Frank first thing when he woke up, or torture him for information. It also made an attempt at escaping much easier. On the other hand, who would hide him in the garden shed and care for his wounds? And most importantly, why?

Frank was so lost in thought that he only noticed someone approaching the shed when he heard steps on the gravel path outside and the lock was opened. Swiftly, Frank closed his eyes, pretending he was still unconscious. From the warmth in his face, he knew sunlight was streaming in as the door opened and a pair of heavy boots stepped in.

Immediately, the door was closed again, the warmth gone from his face, but a whiff of fresh air from outside wafted though the room, carrying with it the distinct scent of a warm summer day.

Calmly, the person who had entered the room walked around, rummaged in some corner and apparently sat down next to Frank's head, judging by the sounds of it. Then, another new scent hit Frank's nose: Chicken broth, plain and delicious, and fresh German rye bread, their scent spreading though the small room like a growing cloud. Despite his intention to stay cool, Frank could feel his mouth begin to water.

How long had he been unconscious and without food? One day? Or more? His body was screaming with hunger.

When unexpectedly, Frank's visitor lifted the plaid, he couldn't suppress a tiny twitch, but apparently, it had been obvious enough to be noticed.

"So we're awake, are we?" a cultivated voice in flawless English asked without any recognizable accent, sounding more amused than anything else.

Feeling too weak for any games, Frank opened his eyes, and, to his utmost surprise and confusion, found Oberst Graf von Biehn sitting at his side, a wide smile on the German's face. Quite a handsome face, Frank had to admit, with intelligent green eyes and straight blond hair.

Handsome if you liked Aryan poster boys, that was.

"Just as I thought," the Oberst added with a soft sigh, then asked, "Are you alright?"

Frank's mind still struggled with the fact that the man whose manor he should have been searching for was sitting right next to him, his dark blond hair and charismatic features exactly matching the photographs Frank had been shown at his mission briefing. And to top things off, von Biehn wore his gray Wehrmacht uniform, full regalia except for the hat, a whole set of medals dangling from his chest, looking lean and fit and inappropriately dashing.

"What is as you thought?" Frank croaked coarsely, cursing himself instantly as he realized he had just given away the fact that he did understand and speak English indeed.

"Your eyes," the Nazi officer replied with a cocky smile. "They're just as beautiful as the rest of you had led me to believe."

For a long moment, Frank could do nothing but blink in utter bewilderment. He had never thought of himself as anything but plain, and why a German officer would consider him "beautiful," of all things, was completely beyond him. Dark haired and athletic, he might pass as handsome, but beautiful? That just didn't make sense.

Maybe it was just a mistake on von Biehn's side, speaking in a language foreign to him. Probably it was.

"*Hier, Süßer,*" von Biehn said after a moment of silence. "I have brought you some food. It would be a shame to let it go cold, and as you seem to be well enough now, you could relieve me of the boring task of spoon-feeding you once again."

Frank still failed to get any hold on the situation. Why on earth did von Biehn call him *Süßer*, sweetie? What did he miss?

But in the end, his growling stomach made the decision for him, and so he nodded a vague consent. In helpless amazement, he watched as the German carefully raised the back of Frank's recliner into a more sitting position, smiling all the time at his involuntary guest.

"Here," von Biehn said as he handed a plate of steaming soup to Frank. "Watch out, it's still fairly hot."

Hot or not, the soup smelled good enough to justify a burned mouth, and by all accounts, that wouldn't much worsen Frank's physical situation anyway. As hasty as his somewhat delicate condition allowed, Frank wolfed down the first spoonfuls of soup, halting only when a wave of fuzzy warmth spread throughout his body.

Slowly, his mind kicked back into gear, and one by one, the things von Biehn had said came back to him.

"You've fed me?" Frank asked, disbelieving. "How long was I gone?"

The Oberst thought for a moment, then answered.

"This is the morning of your third day here. I was already getting a bit worried about you."

"Worried?" Frank took another spoonful of the soup before he went on. "About what? That I'd die on you before you've had time to question me?"

A half-suppressed smirk spread on von Biehn's face, and to Frank's ever-growing confusion, he could have sworn it was less cruelty but indecency he saw in the other man's features. "Well, definitely not in the way you think."

An awkward silence spread between them, von Biehn looking at Frank with a certain fascination, as Frank returned the look with intense confusion. Then, finally, Frank asked the question that had been bugging him the most.

"How'd you guess my language?"

Again, the same smirk, this time wider, though. Leaning back in the small garden chair he had pulled next to the recliner for himself, von Biehn explained.

"Look, you're wearing an outfit that is perfect for an everyday person here in the area. Except that most of it was manufactured in Bohemia, and no decent person here would buy any such stuff. Then, even if, such person would hardly be found unconscious in the mud, attached to a US army parachute with a dismantled sniper rifle on his chest, would he?"

Frank just stared at the man. He knew well enough that his own affliction made him sometimes hear things in the words other men said merely by wishful thinking. His love for men had been a well-kept secret for most of his life, and Frank harbored no intentions whatsoever to change that.

Von Biehn was an attractive man, handsome and virile in his uniform in all the wrong ways. Or the right ways, depending on the point of view.

But he was still the enemy, and Frank for the life of him couldn't figure out why he was imagining von Biehn flirting with him. And why on earth *should* von Biehn be hitting on him? As far as Frank knew, love between two men was even more stigmatized among the Nazi than everywhere else. Or had Frank done something to encourage von Biehn's attitude? Had he been talking while he had been unconscious? Or was it just an attempt by von Biehn to unsettle his prisoner, trying to see how Frank would react? After all, von Biehn didn't seem like a person who was so insecure in a foreign language that he made such a mistake.

Whatever the reasons, Frank was profoundly wary of him. If von Biehn had suddenly sprouted fangs and horns, Frank wouldn't even have flinched.

"And if the parachute and the rifle wouldn't have been enough, *Süßer*," von Biehn said as he leaned forward and explicitly mimed sniffing at Frank's throat, "your aftershave is only available on the US market."

"Stop calling me that," Frank snarled, but von Biehn only grinned. It might be a nice thing to call a gal "sweetie," but for a man, that was plain condescending.

"No, I won't." Von Biehn's smile mellowed for a heartbeat, changing into an expression one might have taken for genuine care and affection if that just hadn't been so utterly impossible. "Eat. I still have things to do."

"Why the hell do you help me?" Frank asked, still too confused and groggy to think of any less blunt attempt at solving this riddle.

"Now, isn't that pretty obvious?" There it was again, that indecent ring to the German's voice. And this time, Frank was sure he wasn't just imagining things. It didn't make any sense. "See, I was standing on my balcony two nights ago, having a late drink, as I heard a plane passing. Which, in itself, wasn't something too unusual, but it wasn't on the standard course and didn't really sound like one of our machines. And then, like a gift from heaven, there comes a magnificent bird of prey with a broken wing plummeting down from the sky, hitting the ground right next to my favorite fishing spot. So I thought, let's have a look. And what I found definitely looked more like a present than anything else. Admittedly, it was a bit battered and muddy. But it still felt like someone upstairs had finally recognized the hard work I do down here and sent me some beautiful angel to share my lonely nights with."

"In your dreams!!" Frank hissed reflexively. So he definitely wasn't imagining things!

Von Biehn smiled sadly, suddenly all flirtation gone from his voice.

"You're here to kill someone, but probably not me. I'm far from being important enough in your government's eyes, at least on my own. So they have taken you from Chicago — where by your accent I assume you are from — put you through training, several missions, as your countless scars tell me, at least one of them in the desert, judging by the sunburn scars on your shoulders, and then dropped you out of a plane over the Spreewald to infiltrate the meeting to be held here in a few days and kill some of my guests; probably good, old Joseph Goebbels among the first of them. Am I right so far?"

Frank only managed to stare blankly at this frighteningly accurate analysis of the situation. He had been ordered to kill von Biehn, though, but only if there were no other, more interesting targets available.

"Don't bother answering," von Biehn said with a dismissive gesture of his hand. "But I can tell you that this meeting is not going to take place as planned. Instead, it'll be about two weeks later, as some other, more important guests have announced their interest in joining the already austere company that will gather here."

"If you are so goddamn sure of why I am here," Frank managed to ask acerbically without one bit of the insecurity he felt showing in his voice. "Shouldn't you feel honor-bound to stop me instead of nursing me back to health?"

"*Süßer*," von Biehn said with no smile at all, "Ever wondered if I might feel honor-bound to kill your targets myself?"

Speechless, Frank remained frozen on his recliner as Oberst von Biehn stood up and walked over to the garden shed's door.

"Don't leave the shed. I have staff running about the manor, and I don't think I could protect you if one of them saw you. Now eat your soup; I'll have a look after you later this afternoon."

And with those words, the German left, leaving behind a completely stunned Captain Hawthorne with a plate of cooling chicken soup in his lap.

Chapter 3
Getting Closer

September 1946, Nuremberg, Palace of Justice, prison wing

Frank had never before believed that the most frightening thing about a prison could be the fact that it was so immaculately clean. But right now, walking down the corridor to the cell where Johann was imprisoned, all the shiny neatness made his skin crawl.

White walls looking like they had been painted only a few days ago. Glossy gray metal doors, gray railings and a floor covered with spotlessly shiny light gray linoleum completed the picture.

As they walked, Elias' shoes clacked on the ground beside him, the sounds echoing throughout the large atrium, driving home with full force the point that though the place was supposedly brimming with prisoners, it was as silent as a grave. But then again, this prison didn't hold some rabble from the streets, but the former ruling elite of

Nazi Germany. Educated, cultured people who had been embroiled in the worst crimes against humanity the world had ever seen. Every single one of them was responsible for the death of thousands; each one of them was silently waiting in their cells to be found guilty and executed.

"So," Frank said to the lawyer next to him just to stop his morbid thoughts. "How did Johann convince you to defend him?"

"There was very little convincing necessary," Elias replied, a calm smile spreading across his gaunt features.

He'll always look thin to the point of emaciation, Frank realized completely out of context. Elias was skinny, with his sharp nose and large ears that stuck to his head as if they had been placed there as an afterthought. Even his narrow, black suit looked like it was several sizes too large.

But his dark eyes were sparkling with a wit and mirth that belied his frail frame. "He wrote me a plain, official letter asking me to plead his case. And as my new employer knew my story, I was here in Nuremberg within a day."

"That is good to hear. Ever thought of calling yourself as a witness?"

The grin on Elias' face widened even more, gaining a decidedly wicked note. "The trial will still go on for quite a while. And I'm not willing to play my best cards all at once."

Cordially, he patted Frank's arm, his eyes flashing a warm encouragement.

Frank had never figured out if Elias knew what exactly had happened between him and Johann, but the lawyer seemed to have guessed the important parts. It was just like him not to waste a single word on the subject and yet tactfully consider their needs in his actions.

It had been Elias' letter suggesting Frank come over to Germany and stand witness for Johann, and he had most gladly agreed to come. Frank didn't think the decision would have been any different if he had known what trouble it would get him into.

"We're here to see Oberst von Biehn." Elias' clear voice nudged him out of his thoughts. "Here are the papers."

A small table had been set up in the corridor, with a bored-looking GI behind it, another one leaning against the wall close by. Both were armed and smoking some imported Twenty Grand cigarettes that were proudly on display on the desk.

Both were also wearing their MP badges with that certain pride that always made Frank very wary. His job had made him instinctively careful around people proud of their uniforms, and it was unpleasant to see that mentality kicking in among his own people as well.

The young soldier at the impromptu desk sifted through Elias' papers, the frown on his face not really showing if he was just annoyed at them disturbing his calm watch or because the papers were all flawlessly in order.

"Yeah," he said hesitantly after a while. "So, you're his lawyer."

It sounded more like an accusation than anything else, but if Elias cared, he didn't let it show.

"Yes, I am. So would you please...?"

The young soldier gave his colleague a short nod, gesturing him to lead them to Johann's cell. Taking the lead, the second GI walked up a stairway that led to another level of the floors circling the atrium, exuding the same slightly bored annoyance as his colleague at the desk.

"Here you are," he finally said, the cigarette in the corner of his mouth as he stopped in front of one of the countless gray doors and opened its tiny window. "Biehn?" he called into the cell. "Visitors!"

Then he started wrestling with the key chain at his belt, apparently having trouble getting it off its hook.

Once again, Elias seemed utterly unmoved, a faint, polite smile on his face. But Frank was beginning to feel nervous.

After all, this was the first time he would really see Johann again; maybe even privately enough to say hello in the appropriate fashion. And his heart was thumping in his chest, as it hadn't done since... well, since that first evening in Johann's manor.

As the soldier was trying to find the right key on his chain, he left Frank time to look around, trying to find anything to distract himself sufficiently so his palms would stop sweating.

Staring at the door, he noticed it must have been painted at least a hundred times over, for its surface was both perfectly clean and glossy, as well as irregular and knobby in places; giving the impression of something cancerous growing underneath the shiny gray surface.

I really have to get out of here, Frank thought fervently, *else I will go mad in this place.*

In front of them, the GI had managed to open the cell's door, gesturing for the other men to enter with mocking politeness.

To his own surprise, Frank found himself taking in a deep breath before he stepped into the cell.

Apparently, this meeting meant even more to him than he had already thought.

"*Graf von Biehn,*" he heard Elias say as he walked into the cell first, genuine happiness in his voice. "*Schön Sie einmal wieder in Ruhe sprechen zu können.*" So nice to talk to you once again. Yes, Frank's thoughts exactly.

Mentally shoving himself around the corner that until now had kept him out of Johann's field of vision, Frank followed Elias and actually managed a decent expression that was neither the dread of this whole situation nor the mad giggling joy of seeing Johann again.

But the impulse to jump at him and hug him was quenched immediately when Frank saw him sitting at the narrow desk at the cell's wall, still wearing the uniform he had sported in court.

He looked so calm, and so frighteningly... frail. *Where was that crazy, dazzling bastard of a man he had fallen in love with that summer, three years ago?*

"*Hallo, Johann...*" Frank managed, trying hard to find anything intelligent to say in the turmoil of his emotions.

"Hi, Frank. Thank you so much for coming." Johann's voice was soft, and though he still resembled the man Frank had fallen for, at this instant, he seemed utterly alien.

Either trying to resolve the delicate situation or not noticing anything, Elias buzzed through the tiny room, and actually finding a second chair, placed Frank on it to face the former German officer.

"You are still wearing your uniform," Frank said as there was nothing else he could say without risking spilling out all of his heart. "The Wehrmacht is gone, there's no need for it any longer. You could wear civilian clothes now."

"It's the only thing I have."

It took a few heartbeats to let the information sink in, but then a wave of fury rushed through Frank, searing enough to finally get him focused again.

"They don't let you wear anything else?!" Turning around, Frank looked at Elias. "What is the meaning of this, Elias?"

Calm as always, Elias said, "Captain Hawthorne, please. This matter has already been discussed and we all agree upon the way things are handled here."

Luckily, Frank noticed that there was something odd in the way Elias looked at him. Following his eyes, Frank turned around and found the young MP leaning against the cell's door frame, smoking, absent-mindedly fingering his belt-buckle, an insolent smirk on his face.

"What the -" Frank stared at Elias, then at the soldier, then back at Johann. "But you're his goddamn lawyer!"

"Captain Hawthorne." Despite everything, Elias still sounded almost serene. "As I said, we absolutely agree with the local administration's way of running things here. I'll still have to antagonize them often enough, so we shouldn't busy ourselves with such details. And besides, it's not as if we have anything to hide, do we?"

So that's what this was all about.

Wordlessly, Frank stared at Elias, wondering if he truly was unable to get them an unobserved meeting with Johann. But that would have been very unlike him. Given the way Elias had arranged things for them in Italy, once their flight out of Germany had succeeded, Elias should have been able to arrange something like that three times over. So, he must have wanted the local guards to overhear all they said.

But why? All the questions burning inside him would now only make Frank sound as if he was in love with von Biehn.

Which, of course, was the whole point, but that would render him perfectly useless as a witness in his favor. If anything of their relationship would become public, it would make Johann appear even more the perverted, mind-bending Nazi criminal.

Frank could already hear Jackson suggesting that it had been Johann's dangerous skills of subversion that had made him fall for a man in the very first place, and that it was absolutely not Frank's fault at all.

"No, of course not." Suddenly, Frank's voice sounded just as flat and careful as Johann's. Which, given the circumstances, probably explained a lot of things. "Please excuse my outbreak."

Instead of an answer, Elias simply nodded, his eyes full of silent understanding. *How much did that guy know?* Frank asked himself for the thousandth time.

And Johann? He was still looking at Frank, his features without any readable expression. But there was something in his green eyes, a distant glimmer that reminded Frank so much of the daring, impossible sneak he had fallen in love with.

Again, Frank felt his heart thump in his chest, and this time, it was more excitement than angst.

Maybe, and perhaps with a little bit of luck, there was still that mad German in there who loved him since Frank had fallen from the sky "like an angel with a broken wing."

"It is really good to see you again, Captain Hawthorne," Johann finally said, with just enough emotion to make it sound credible, but not enough to make it sound like something important. He was putting on a show. "So tell me, how was your flight?"

"Actually not too bad, Graf von Biehn. It was very nice for a change to leave a plane that's not in the air."

Elias and Johann both laughed politely.

Good heavens, here he was sitting next to the man he had basically thrown away his life for, and all he did was make moderately witty small talk! And nothing promised a quick end to the drama.

No, the charade went on, stretching for what seemed like hours. They were sitting in the tiny cell, listening to Elias chatting animatedly about his younger sister's youngest daughter, who was just about now learning how to open drawers and was making a general mess of her mother's life.

Considering the fact that when they had met the first time, Elias hadn't known if anyone in his family was still alive, this was absolutely great news. But still Frank felt like there were millions of things far more important waiting to be said.

Then, as if the utterly boring talk had finally overwhelmed his sense of duty, the GI at the door gave a deep sigh and left his place for a short walk down the corridor.

Just as if he had waited for that moment all the time, suddenly Johann's knee gently leaned against Frank's. Almost electrified by the unexpected touch, Frank looked up at him, only to find Johann's face beaming with joy.

"Thank you," he whispered, so softly Frank could hardly make out the words. "Thanks for being here, *Süßer.*"

Had he really just said that? Afraid he had heard the words only by wishful thinking, Frank blankly stared at him, his face trying hard to hide a silly grin from ear to ear.

"Hey!" The GI's sharp voice from the door reminded everyone that they were not alone.

Immediately, Johann's features returned to that awful, subdued expression, his knee quitting contact with Frank's almost dangerously slowly.

"I think your time's up now; all things of importance are said. Come on," the GI ordered, more bored than anything. Apparently, he had decided that he couldn't bear one more word about cute, distantly related toddlers.

"Well, Graf von Biehn," Frank said as if concluding an earlier sentence. "I can only say that we absolutely agree in that regard. I hope we can talk further on that subject when we celebrate your release."

Giving Johann a gentle look and a nod, Frank turned around to face the soldier. "We will leave now, I think, and bother you no longer. And you are right, all important things are said."

They were, indeed, and Frank had to pinch his arm till it bled to keep himself from hooting and jumping with joy.

***

August 1943, Spreewald, von Biehn estate

"So how's my favorite brooding angel today?" von Biehn asked playfully as he entered the shed. "Look, I'm bringing you a present and good news."

This man was mad, plainly mad.

"I managed to walk a few steps without fainting today, so I'm quite happy."

It wouldn't help if Frank told him that he had been exercising for the last three days already. Though impressively and colorfully bruised, his ribs had proven not to be broken; in contrary to what the German officer believed.

This, together with Frank's nicely healing sprained ankle, already gave him quite an advantage once he would attempt to flee.

"Now what do you say?"

Blinking at von Biehn without a clue what he was talking of, it took Frank a moment to realize he actually had brought a wheelchair with him. An old, almost antique monstrosity, with the small wheels at the rear, probably something left over from the middle of the last century. It even had a tiny lace doily draped across its neck-rest.

"I say: What the hell do I need a wheelchair for? There's not even space enough in this shed to turn around."

"Hm," von Biehn said and scratched his chin. "Would you rather hobble to the mansion?"

"The mansion? But — what about your staff?"

What was this crazy person up to? And why bring Frank to his mansion?

"There's no staff, at least not for the next few days until the meeting. I sent them away."

There was no guile in his voice, at least none that Frank was able to make out. And anyway, during the last days in his custody, he had basically given up figuring out what von Biehn was thinking.

On the one hand, he looked like the stereotypical German officer, blond, slightly tanned, his green eyes almost passing for blue if one didn't look too close. An expressive face that laughed and frowned often, his aristocratic features offset by the first signs of laughing lines in the corners of his eyes. Constantly wearing his gray Wehrmacht uniform, his jacket unbuttoned only at the most casual occasions. Most of the times, he was even wearing those glistening black gloves that seemed to be all the rage in Aryan fashion.

However, since Frank had awoken in the shed, von Biehn had come to him at least twice each day, bringing food, changing his bandages. Once Frank had awoken and found the German sitting next to him, a soft, slightly embarrassed smile on his face.

Von Biehn even tried to entertain him, in a sweet, kind, and utterly unconvincing way. Somehow, small talk with a high-ranking German Nazi officer just wasn't on Frank's mind.

Especially not as said officer seemed to be harboring intentions Frank was most definitely not going to encourage. Well, at least not as long as it wasn't absolutely vital to his mission. Alright, make that possibly vital to his mission. Without this appalling uniform, von Biehn would look rather strapping, after all.

"No staff?" Frank asked. "Won't that make people suspicious that you sent all your staff away?"

Softly, von Biehn laughed. "You've read my dossier before they kicked you out of your plane. You probably know better what people will think about me than my humble self."

And once more, von Biehn was far too close to the truth for his taste.

"They think you'll just go on being eccentric, as usual. But you're in favor with people sufficiently high up the ranks, so no one will dare to ask questions. Virtually everybody will come to the conclusion that you're doing something you'd like to be kept secret, and as nobody will dare to anger you, most probably they even won't come and spy on you."

"See?" Pushing the wheelchair closer to the recliner Frank was lying on, von Biehn added, "Sometimes, those elitist absolutist systems do have their advantages. Now can you get into the chair on your own or will I have to haul you in?"

"How can you be joking about this?"

"About what? I wasn't joking; if necessary, I can carry you."

"Your system. You sound as if you know what's happening; that not everything is like they tell you."

"Look, *Süßer*, if you got the choice between laughing and crying, always pick laughter. There are already more than enough tears in this world."

For a long moment, awkward silence grew between them. Everything in Frank longed to press this subject further, to find out why a member of the Nazi elite as renowned as von Biehn spoke like that. But then again, Frank hardly knew him, and this subject just seemed too delicate. Never argue with a madman, and that von Biehn was as far away from sane as the sun from the moon was without question.

"Why are you doing this?" Frank asked anyway, studying von Biehn's face for any hint to his motives.

"Depends on what you mean with 'this'," he replied, smirking. He gestured for Frank to get into the wheelchair, and there didn't seem to be any reason not to indulge him.

That was, no reason beyond the plain fact that it was complete madness, but that seemed to be the motto of this whole mission. And after all, Frank really wanted to get out of this cramped little space, to get some air and see something different. So, he carefully heaved himself out of the recliner, making sure von Biehn didn't get any impression of how good his condition actually was.

"Ready?" Frank was asked as von Biehn left his position behind the wheelchair and draped a dark blanket over Frank's legs, carefully tucking in the corners so they wouldn't catch in the wheels. Maybe it was all a setup, a ruse to make Frank feel secure and to spill some secrets he wouldn't ever have divulged even under torture. But then von Biehn must have been an amazing actor. He seemed genuinely sweet when it came to caring for Frank.

"*Achtung, Süßer*, here we go!" Apparently in a splendid mood, von Biehn pushed Frank out of the shed, and despite everything, he really was glad to be outside for a change.

And what a lovely outside that was. The completely overgrown shed was huddled against the trunk of a giant oak, its low branches gnarled and sturdy. All around, similarly ancient trees were standing, mostly beeches and oaks, the ground covered with a neatly kept lawn.

It looked like a park, complete with raked white gravel paths and probably fake Greek marble statues tastefully sprinkled in between. Handsome, male Greek gods, to be precise. Huge rhododendron hedges blocked the sight, some of them easily over ten feet tall, but Frank could already see the red-tiled roof of a mansion ahead of them.

Despite the gleaming sun, it was pleasantly cool in the shade. Von Biehn's shoes and the wheels of the chair crunched noisily on the gravel, and apart from a few songbirds, all was calm.

There was no water to be seen, yet a constant murmur was in the air, and Frank could almost smell the river all around them.

Frank had read about this area, the Spreewald, when he prepared for this mission. But he had never thought it would be this... nice. The Spreewald was a section where one of Germany's biggest rivers divided up into countless tiny streams and creeks, creating a huge, slow flowing network of shallow water with just as many forested islands in between. And even though it was a hassle to get here and the building ground usually was no better than your average swamp, it was no small wonder that quite a share of the Nazi elite's most important people had set up their elusive hideaways here.

Except for the current owners and all the people around, Frank could really get used to living here.

"It's beautiful, isn't it?" von Biehn asked as he noticed Frank's silent awe at the lush vegetation. "You should see it in May and June when the rhododendrons are in full bloom."

"It's wonderful," Frank admitted honestly. "Like a botanical garden."

For a moment, neither of them spoke, and Frank wondered if ever he would be able to come back and see the hedges covered all over with bundles of red and white blossoms so thick there wouldn't be any leaves left to see.

Well, most probably not. They were at war, after all, and even if he was to survive the coming days, who knew if this place wouldn't be bombed down to rubble in the near future.

Finally, they came around a bend in the path, and the mansion rose in classic elegance ahead of them. It was smaller than Frank had expected, ninety, maybe a hundred feet on its longest side. But it exuded the same calm quality the whole place was reverberating with, vine and ivy covering a good portion of its pale yellow walls.

While von Biehn pushed Frank up a ramp that apparently had been built ages ago, he wondered how von Biehn could live here on his own. Of course, he had servants, but it struck Frank as odd nevertheless that there was no one else, not even the almost obligatorily pregnant Aryan wife.

He truly must be close with the people in high places to be able to lead such a questionable lifestyle. There had been people made to silently disappear for less.

Inside, the mansion was dark and calm, high ceilinged rooms with tall windows, antique furniture on glistening, polished wooden floors. This place was old, Frank realized, with generations of the same families having lived here since, well, probably long before the French Revolution. And it didn't give Frank the impression that there had been a change in ownership lately.

Giving his host a long, intrigued glance, Frank wondered if maybe that was the key to this mystery. He was "Graf von Biehn," Count of Biehn, after all, and though noble titles didn't mean much these days, it might just hint that he felt a responsibility for his country that ran deeper than political fashion.

"Now why are you looking at me like this, *Süßer?*" von Biehn asked, smiling. "Have you finally noticed I'm not the monster they told you I am?"

"No. I'm just wondering which side you are on."

"On the side of my country, dear, always on the side of my country."

He was fully aware that he hadn't really answered Frank's question with that, and he knew Frank knew.

Heavens, I'm here to kill, not to think, Frank thought with exasperation.

"Watch out," von Biehn softly reminded Frank as he turned the wheelchair from the hallway into what took Frank a few seconds to identify as an elevator. At least, it looked like some kind of wrought iron, counterweight and rope-driven antique monstrosity that apparently was meant to get people from one floor to another without the need of stairs, so it qualified as an elevator.

"Quite a nifty mechanism," von Biehn remarked while pulling both of them upwards along the thick rope that ran through the corner of the box they were now in. "My blessed grandmother was unable to walk for the last two decades of her long life, just as we were unable to convince her to move somewhere more accessible. But her stubbornness, my gain. Now I have all the amenities needed to make a hobbled guest feel at home."

Despite himself, Frank had to smile at von Biehn's cordial manner. Though he was still utterly unconvinced of his motivation, Frank was beginning to believe von Biehn truly was trying to help.

"Thanks," he said, earning a soft laugh.

"Don't thank me." Opening the elevator door that now led to the first floor's hallway, Johann looked at Frank with suddenly no mirth at all left in his eyes. "Don't. There will come a moment I will ask you to return my kindness, and I'm not sure if you'll still feel grateful afterwards."

Of course, there was one thing that prominently jumped into Frank's mind, and his disbelieving embarrassment must have shown in his face, for suddenly von Biehn broke into laughter again, pushing the wheelchair out of the elevator.

"Oh, my God, no!" Laughing so hard he couldn't speak for a moment, he continued pushing Frank along another long corridor. "No, *Süßer*, not that. I was talking more serious business, and definitely less pleasant. Though, just for the record, I would definitely feel most honored if I could win your favor in the original sense of the term as well."

Well, at least now the cards were out officially, but it utterly failed to make Frank feel any less uncomfortable.

"And please don't say anything right now," von Biehn added immediately as Frank opened his mouth. "I know quite well when I'm trying to catch a distant star, but that doesn't stop me trying, either."

Abandoning Frank's wheelchair for a second, he opened a door to the right. "And about the business part, we will talk tomorrow."

In this case, there truly was nothing left for Frank to say, and with nothing more than a silent shrug, he let himself be pushed into the huge bathroom through the open door.

"What..." Frank mumbled in surprise, but von Biehn just smiled at him.

"You're smelling, *Süßer*, and I'm not going to dine with you like that." Turning on the hot water for the tub, he continued, "And I think, apart from the obvious, a bath would help you tremendously to get back to health soon." He then pointed to a small pile of clothes and added, "I've gotten you some new clothes; there's a shaver and all else you might need."

Looking at Frank still sitting motionless in the wheelchair, von Biehn frowned, softly asking, "Will you get into the tub on your own or do you want me to help you?"

Yes, and help Frank undress too, of course. *To hell with secrecy*, Frank thought, he wanted a bath without a Nazi officer fingering him all over.

"No, I think I'll manage on my own. Thank you."

"Of course." Von Biehn actually managed to look almost as if he wasn't disappointed. "If you continue down the hallway, you'll come to my library. I'll be waiting there for you."

And with hardly an audible sound, he closed the door.

When Frank was finally alone, he stood up from the wheelchair and walked around the bathroom in careful steps. From the bathtub, thick clouds of steam were already rising, and once again, he wondered what a lovely place this would have been if things had only been a little different. It all looked as if right out of the last century, with the black and white square tiles diagonally on the floor, the immense white enamel bathtub with its brazen lion's feet.

Taking off his pullover, Frank took a deep breath as the first, shy fingers of moist air touched his skin.

In one thing, von Biehn had been right after all. He was in dire need of a bath. Frank carefully unwrapped his bandaged chest, cursing softly as he moved his left arm with too much vigor.

He wasn't seriously hurt, but really should better remember he was far from being fit. Yet.

Waiting until the tub had the right temperature, a tiny detail caught Frank's attention. On a small shelf above the sink, there was a small pot of hair wax. British wax, the kind that gave the Brylcreem Boys their name. About the last item Frank would have expected here.

And if that wasn't strange enough, there also was a chunk of sinfully expensive Sicilian lemon soap by the tub. The original stuff, not the modern synthetic imitations.

His curiosity triggered, Frank snooped around a little, and found wonders upon wonders. Persian after-shave, heavy with the tangy scent of pomegranate oil. Ground Tahitian nutshells, hand-balm with herbs, produced in some obscure French monastery.

This definitely was no average Aryan household, not even by far. This man must have traveled the world, and apparently, he had found something he liked in every corner of it. And if Frank was not utterly mistaken, a man with such experiences could hardly be convinced by the one-dimensional, if compelling, lure of national or racial superiority.

Giving a deep sigh, Frank undressed completely, deciding that whatever mysteries were lingering in this place, there would be enough time to solve them once he had taken a bath. There was a good chance this would be the very last hot tub of his life, and he would thoroughly enjoy it.

Chapter 4
Spying for Beginners

September 1946, Nuremberg

"Von Biehn!" Cursing under his breath, Chief attorney Jackson paced his office, so concentrated he didn't notice that his wispy hair was in disarray. "Does he really think hiring a Jew for his defense will make him look any less guilty?"

In his corner, Benedict nodded silently. He had no clue what precisely was the point of his employer's latest outburst, and he sure as hell wouldn't say so. Jackson had an uncertain temper, and lying low had proven the best way to remain unscathed if he was in one of his moods.

"You know, Benedict, what makes me really nervous about the whole thing?" Jackson asked, waiting only long enough for his aide to shake his head before he continued. "That the Jewish community is not protesting. That this little Italian lawyer isn't buried in paper six feet deep. They protest against everything these days, so why not this case?"

Still pacing up and down the open space in front of his huge desk, the chief attorney of the Nuremberg trials gestured wildly with his arms, as if arguing to unseen audiences. His unbuttoned vest revealed a coffee stain from earlier this morning on his shirt, and Jackson couldn't have cared less. He was upset, to no end, as he always was when there were obvious details he didn't know.

Unfortunately, this kind of situation seemed to be commonplace when dealing with von Biehn.

"I mean," Jackson continued his passionate argument to no one in particular, "we've all read the files. If we were to pick the twenty most important movers and shakers of the Third Reich, he would be among them every time. Heavens, we even have confirmed information that it was von Biehn who developed the pivotal stratagems of the Grevenbroich manifesto, even though he never claimed credit!"

Seeing nothing but polite blankness in Benedict's face, he frowned deeply, angered at the obvious lack of common knowledge.

"The Grevenbroich manifesto was the final paper of a semi-public study on how to maximize efficiency in both the government and the army. It suggested groundbreaking changes that were only implemented after strong initial resistance, once again with von Biehn lobbying it in the front row. Since then, every Reichsmark they spent got them almost forty percent more than before. This bloody paper saved them more money than they could have looted in all of Europe."

Knowing that the impromptu lecture was now finished, Benedict nodded, demurely taking notes.

"Read that manifesto, you'll see how close genius and madness are at times."

At last, Jackson seemed to get a little calmer, the strain of the last weeks finally showing. Wiping back his hair, the attorney took a deep breath before he continued in a much more composed fashion.

"Let's get back once more to this lawyer," he proposed, clearly talking more to himself to sort out his thoughts than to Benny. "Elias Blumenstein. Do we know anything about his background?"

"Only the official stuff, sir," Benedict replied nonetheless. "Had a practice in Potsdam before the Nazis closed it, went underground when his properties were confiscated and fled to Italy during the war. He reunited with his family and now lives in... Florence, I think."

"Does he have a proper job?" Jackson asked, his hands folded at the small of his back as he stared out of the window onto the rain-drenched street below.

"If you consider being junior partner of one of Florence's eldest law-firms a proper job, then yes, sir."

Shooting a glance and a wry grin at his assistant, Jackson nodded slowly. Even though he wasn't one to dole out compliments to his employees, he acknowledged when Benny did a good job. He had often enough told Benny that he considered him far too soft to ever make anything else but a lawyer's aide. But Benny also knew that if Jackson wouldn't consider him perfect for that job, he wouldn't be here right now.

"There's something so rotten it should be visible a mile away," Jackson went on grumbling, once again staring out onto the street. "Von Biehn had a widely known history of collecting objects that had been confiscated from Jewish households, buying them at horrendous prices. Every Rabbi from Kiev to New York should preach to have him burned at the stake! But nothing, not a word — are we sure von Biehn's assets were frozen as soon as we could get a hold of them?"

"As sure as we can be, sir."

"Alright," Jackson stated in his voice that indicated an abrupt change of subject. Apparently, there weren't any new thoughts to be found on the Nazi's Jewish lawyer. "That witness Blumenstein brought up yesterday. Our mysterious Captain Hawthorne... "

"Sir, our request on his file was answered this morning," Benedict injected, swiftly gathering up the pivotal parts in his mind. "A highly decorated war hero, special ops, undercover missions the kind that movies are made from."

Nodding in confirmation of already well-known facts, Jackson returned to looking out of the window while Benedict continued.

"He has a sister living in California, no other relatives, no wife." Knowing that the best was still to come, Benedict paused for a heartbeat to make sure he had his superior's full attention, then he added matter-of-factly, "And he's expecting to be demoted and discharged from the military service for appearing here at court."

"What?!" Jackson snapped, almost bellowing with surprise, most obviously glad that there was something new in this unwieldy case. "He was ordered not to stand witness?"

"Precisely, sir." Benedict nodded, causing a strand of his hair to fall into his face. One of these days, he promised himself, he had to get a crew cut, as much as he loathed it. He loved his hair as it was, brown and wavy and long enough in the front to reach down to the tip of his nose if he didn't keep it neatly combed back all the time. On the other hand, it set him apart from all the butch guys in their uniforms running around the place, and that wasn't necessarily a good thing. Jackson considered Benny's haircut a vain folly, and had said so more than once already.

"So Captain Hawthorne was under direct orders to stay away from the trials and he came anyway?" Jackson asked with genuine excitement, beaming with the joy of having new information to put into the larger picture. "But why doesn't he face a court-martial?"

"Same question I asked myself, sir. Probably his officers know more than we do."

"Of course they do," Jackson snapped, a note of bitterness creeping into his voice. "And once again, they won't tell."

"Maybe they're holding back their reaction until the outcome of the trial is clear. It wouldn't look too good to court-martial a hero for trying to save a man proven innocent by these trials."

Slowly, almost menacingly, Jackson turned around to stare at Benedict. He could have sworn there was red fire in his superior's eyes in that moment. Coldly and treacherously calm, Jackson then asked. "Mister de Havilland, with all due respect, do you know more than I do? If so, I would strongly like to know what makes you believe that there is even a remote trace of a chance that we won't win our case?"

"I - I -" Benedict stammered as he faced his employer's wrath without warning. "Sir, I don't know anything more. But... this Captain Hawthorne struck me as a person of integrity, and if he's here against orders, he must believe in what he does."

"He struck you as a nice person." His voice seeping with sarcasm, Jackson grinned coldly. "I pray to God that there will never come a day I will have to rely on your skills as a lawyer."

"Yes, sir," Benedict mumbled, deeply embarrassed by the mirthless comment. Jackson had a knack for making him feel inferior and useless, Benedict found once more. And it angered him to no end that it still hurt so much.

"You're just too soft, Benedict," Jackson continued, making Benedict cringe even more. "But maybe there's finally something we can do to put you to good use."

Torn between the strong urge to hit his employer with some heavy object and grinning like a happy puppy that finally got a kind word out of its master, Benedict looked up again. Jackson stood there, a fiendish glint in his eyes, nodding as if congratulating himself on a great idea.

"You know, being the little scribe you are, there's basically no chance Hawthorne will have ever noticed you," he explained, seemingly oblivious to the fact that he was neatly continuing to assault Benedict's ego. "You're a nice chap, and only a little younger than Hawthorne. Couldn't you go out, try to find our rogue Captain and make friends with him? Have a beer, let him act the hero he is and tell you stories of the war you could never participate in — maybe then we'll get something more useful out of you than just that he's a decent guy."

Sitting on his chair in the corner of the room, Benedict nodded, not really knowing what kind of task this was and how the hell he would achieve it. But he would try, and try hard, that much was sure.

"Great, great," Jackson concluded, rubbing his hands that were growing cold with concentration. "Now who's next on our list? Any new witnesses announced?"

***

August 1943, Spreewald, von Biehn manor

However pleasant the hot bath was, it couldn't last forever.

And he couldn't lock himself up in the bathroom for the rest of the night either. His life depended on von Biehn's prolonged interest in him. And he didn't really see himself risking such a fucked-up mission on his mere unwillingness to entertain his target's fancies.

And a rather handsome target, at that.

Frowning at this last thought, Frank gave himself a last glance in the bathroom's mirror. Was there actually anything he wouldn't do to ensure he'd fulfill his mission? Right then, he couldn't think of one thing he could name; but was sure there was, hoped there would be.

The thought that he couldn't really stop himself at anything to fulfill an order he had been given frightened him. The feeling was all too similar to the utter devotion he saw in the enemies' eyes every time. Struck by one of those unpleasant moments of clarity, he wondered where the difference was between the good guys and the bad guys if their means were all just born out of perceived necessity and their goals by the unquestioned orders they had been given.

Hopefully, this war would be over soon.

Giving his mirror image a shy smile, Frank brushed off those thoughts. He was here on a mission, and all else he could ponder afterwards. Right now, all that mattered was the dinner with his slightly mad captor and staying alive. Maybe he would be able to glean some useful information out of von Biehn at the same time.

Inspecting what he saw in front of him, he had to admit that von Biehn had demonstrated superb taste in picking his new outfit, little surprise there.

Dark trousers and a pullover; a soft, large pullover a few shades lighter than his eyes. As he wasn't wearing a shirt underneath, he could see his collarbones peeking out from under the neckband. A sight he surprisingly found reminded him of the fact that despite whatever clothing he wore, he was still naked underneath.

A notion von Biehn had surely been thinking about as well.

Looking at his image in the mirror again, Frank wondered what von Biehn was seeing in him.

Did he really consider him beautiful? In a way, that notion was laughable, but then von Biehn had said so the very moment Frank had woken up in the shed, when it had been about the worst possible moment for such a move if this was all just a ruse.

With his dark brown hair in a neat crew cut, a rather angular face and a sharp nose, Frank assumed he was handsome in a plain, masculine way. He was broad-shouldered and athletic, yes. But beautiful? Surely not. Maybe his eyes. Frank had always liked their dark color, somewhere between chocolate and coffee, though to him they looked far too cautious and distrustful to be attractive.

Von Biehn really must be desperate, Frank thought with a mean chuckle.

Shaking his head, Frank heaved himself into the monstrous black wheelchair that von Biehn had presumably inherited from his late grandmother. Down the hallway and into the study, von Biehn had said, there he would be waiting for them to dine together.

Opening the bathroom door proved a little difficult, for Frank hadn't expected the wheelchair to be as bulky as it looked; nor had he anticipated the door's mechanism to be quite so clunky. But with a little effort, he managed to get out of the bathroom without standing up.

All the better, he thought. *As long as I act a little clumsy, von Biehn actually might think me weaker than I am.*

Out in the corridor, there was little mistaking the way he was expected to go. It had been late afternoon when von Biehn got him here from his shed, and now the sun was already setting low on the horizon.

Of the many doors leading out of the hallway, only one opened to a lit room. Soft, slightly scratchy music pearled through the air, and as he was rolling through the long corridor, Frank wondered once again what this place would have been like in a different time.

The music playing was some opera, though Frank couldn't have said which one. It was a beautiful woman's voice singing in Italian, and that was as far as his common knowledge would get him. At least, it definitely wasn't Wagner.

Entering the library, Frank saw that it was more a large living room rather than a study, just with a desk instead of a three-piece-suite. A few candles shed gentle golden light, reflecting on dark wooden shelves that were filled with old books behind stained-glass doors. A little to his left, an array of tall windows and a narrow door led out onto a large balcony overlooking the treetops of the Spreewald.

Leaning against the railing of the balcony, von Biehn was standing, a wide glass of red wine in his hand, looking out into the colorful sunset. Next to him, there was an old gramophone playing the music Frank had already heard in the hallway, and not far off, a table draped in white linen was set for two, complete with a silver candle holder.

The whole setup made Frank blink in disbelief. It was beautiful, romantic, and utterly absurd.

Von Biehn had, for the first time ever in Frank's presence, taken off his Wehrmacht uniform, and now sported a pair of sable slacks and a white shirt, leaving the top two buttons open. The outfit looked like he had just come in from the tennis court or the putting range, all lean and fit, slightly tanned and radiantly healthy. Despite everything, Frank had to admit that von Biehn looked striking.

This wasn't the first time another man was trying to seduce Frank. Nor would it be the first time that he gave in to his suitor. If one's life was set up around killing other people on order, the common teachings of morality after a time inevitably felt as petty and as much open to negotiation as the fifth commandment. Frank knew that something was wrong with him in that regard, but in all honesty he couldn't bring himself to care. Loving men didn't *feel* wrong; all the contrary. And he enjoyed sleeping with them all the more when they were as sure about themselves as von Biehn.

Still, this time, something was different. It would be the first time that Frank would consciously let his job command his sexual life, and he didn't feel comfortable about that. Also, there was the nagging thought that maybe there was a little more to his eagerness to get into the Nazi's bed. Von Biehn was at least a little crazy, but in a kind of way that Frank found more and more fascinating.

Before he could hang on to his thoughts, Johann finally noticed him sitting in his wheelchair, waiting in front of the small step that led onto the balcony.

"So you've finally found your way here!" he exclaimed warmly, setting down his glass. "Wait a second, let me help you."

As if having worked with handicapped people all his life, von Biehn expertly maneuvered Frank out of his wheelchair and over the step. Slowly helping him hobble across the balcony, he took his time staring rather unabashed at his guest. Finally, when he had Frank seated at the table, von Biehn gave him a subdued smile, his eyes sparkling.

"The pullover suits you," he commented evenly.

"Thanks..." Should he go on and play the bristling porcupine, Frank wondered, or would it be better to act a little less aloof, interested even? Without really deciding on one or another of those options, he just went with the truth. "You also look good... in different clothing."

He had wanted to say "without your uniform," but in a way that hadn't felt the right thing. It wasn't the uniform that made Frank squirm each time he saw it on von Biehn. Rather it was what it symbolized; which, in the end, made it one and the same again.

"I'm on holiday today, so there's no reason to wear that dreaded thing," von Biehn replied as if he was reading Frank's thoughts. Fetching a dark bottle from a narrow table at the nearby wall, the officer asked him if he would like some red wine, which Frank accepted.

This whole scenario is utterly absurd, Frank thought again. Sitting there, with von Biehn filling his glass like a waiter in a first class restaurant, he was strongly aware of how grotesquely incredible this moment was.

Not only were they officially mortal enemies in a war as entrenched as the world had ever seen; he was also basically in the very heart of his enemy's country, an uncovered assassin on top. Sitting here, viewing a late August sunset, on the roof terrace of an old mansion overlooking the forest while having a romantic candlelight dinner was so much beyond reason it felt hysterically comical.

Only, it wasn't.

There was such a calm sincerity to von Biehn's mad but nonetheless charming attitude that, more and more, Frank found it hard not to like him at least a little bit. But luckily, it was also von Biehn himself who brought back to Frank's mind who he was and where.

"One thing I always wondered about you Americans," von Biehn noted abruptly, gesturing with his own glass of wine. "Why do you have to shave your heads like that? You look like some kind of prisoner."

Rather stunned, it took Frank quite some time to get his thoughts back on track. He never had given much thought to his haircut, but being compared to a prisoner wasn't exactly something he wanted to hear. Especially given his currently undefined status here.

"Isn't that what I am?" Frank finally asked, maybe a little snappier than he had intended to.

"No, actually you are not," was von Biehn's surprisingly smooth reply. "Consider yourself my guest, and before you ask, yes, you are indeed free to go. Though, we both know that would be rather stupid, which is one thing you are not."

Johann closed his little speech with a bittersweet smile that included so much of everything and nothing at all at the same time that Frank was plainly confused.

"Your soldiers also have short hair," Frank stated in a clumsy attempt to divert from his status as "guest."

"Yes, but not like... this." Again pointing vaguely at Frank's haircut with his wineglass, von Biehn's face was a riddling mix between serious repulsion and tongue-in-cheek small-talk nonsense. "It looks uncivilized. Even soldiers are human beings and should therefore be able to see further than mere practical necessities."

Faced with such categorical rejection of something as peripheral as a haircut, Frank could only blink and smile blankly. If this was von Biehn's idea of romantic talk, there was little wonder he was living here alone.

Noticing how his last comment had left his guest at a loss, von Biehn smiled apologetically, now taking his turn at inelegantly changing the subject.

"I hope you are hungry," he said, pointing at the side-table. "As usual when I am cooking for guests, I have made far too much."

"You cook?" Frank asked at this truly unexpected information, but then again, he should have known to expect the unexpected with von Biehn.

"Only a little. Just what I picked up here and there," von Biehn explained, smirking at Frank's obvious surprise, adding with a wink, "It's a tremendous advantage when trying to seduce someone..."

Now that definitely was a good reason why a Wehrmacht officer would learn how to cook, Frank thought, barely able to keep himself from snorting sarcastically. And yet, taking into account how much Frank was looking forward to some good food, it wasn't all that far-fetched a notion for a man of von Biehn's inclinations. Just what on earth made von Biehn so sure he would find a partner equally inclined in Frank?

Still smiling, von Biehn presented the food on the sidetable with the flair of a French maître de, his hands painting images into the air. Whatever could be said about von Biehn, he definitely loved food, that much was sure.

"We're having linguine tonight, and as I didn't know if you'd like the Bella Maria sauce, I made a second one, so you can choose. It's a cream sauce with garlic and... *Flußkrebse*, what's the name... think tiny lobsters, just out of the rivers here."

Smiling at Frank as hopefully as a little boy might on Christmas when presenting his self-made gift to his mother, von Biehn actually looked adorable, as inconceivable as that thought might have sounded on first instance.

Frank had to admit that a growing part of him was thinking of von Biehn as genuinely charming, if a little irritating. Getting to know him better on romantic terms was still an absurd and dangerous notion, but then again, what was life without a little risk?

It might turn out to be an interesting evening, after all.

Chapter 5
Connecting the Dots

September 1946, Nuremberg, pub Zum Guldenen Stern

"... and as you can surely imagine, this is not at all going to sit well with Jackson," Elias concluded his explanations, folding his napkin as if to ritually finish both talk and dinner.

"Of course it isn't. But Jackson isn't one to sit down and gnash his teeth," Frank replied, still ponderously playing with the last bits of his meal. "He's going to do something about it, and in this case, 'it' is going to be you and me."

Elias only nodded gravely, leaning back with his mug of beer in one hand. For a long moment, neither of the two men spoke, the din of the pub they were having dinner at washing over their table like the sound of waves.

In silence, Frank finished his "*Würstel und Kraut*," tiny fried sausages and sour white cabbage, which he had genuinely been looking forward to eating since returning to Germany. It was one of those dishes he wouldn't recommend eating anywhere in the world except here and maybe in what currently had become eastern France once again.

But this time, even the admittedly good food wouldn't improve his mood, it seemed. The meeting with Johann in prison had left Frank giddy and exhausted at the same time, and desperately wondering what he could actually do to help him.ND Dinner with Elias now had him disillusioned, cold and miserable.

It wasn't going too well for Johann, as the lawyer had put it carefully. Whatever they might think of him personally wasn't going to have any weight in court, and actual proof of his deeds was hardly to be found. At least, that was when one was looking for deeds that wouldn't lead to a death sentence.

Of things against Johann, though, there was ample evidence anywhere one cared to look. Too often had his name been mentioned by highest circles, too often had he been recommended by the wrong people. That Johann had pursued a completely different agenda of his own had been his secret — a secret he had ensured would leave no trace. And in this case, no trace meant no evidence. No evidence meant little hope.

Of course, Elias had been positive about all this, talking a lot about Jackson and his tactics and legal details. But he hadn't been able to distract Frank from the core problem: There simply was no real proof for Johann being anything but the spotless, soulless, perfect Aryan mastermind everybody had taken him for.

"So," Frank asked as he had finished his dinner as well. "What do we do next?"

"Nothing but what we have talked about," Elias replied calmly. "You appear at court again when Jackson has questions, and I will see to finding more witnesses brave enough to testify." Giving a sad little smile, he added, "Former Nazi officers aren't very popular these days."

Snorting bitterly, Frank nodded. If truth was a fickle thing, justice was even more ephemeral.

"Don't worry too much," Elias tried to calm him. Leaning forward, he added softly, "You can't imagine how much it means for Johann to have you here. In that way, you already have helped so much."

"It doesn't feel like I'm doing anything useful. In contrary, I feel like I'm a danger to him."

"Nah. Don't underestimate the power of an honest soul." Elias actually sounded as if he believed in such naive nonsense. "And in the end, it will be the judges who decide."

"And that is a good thing?" Frank asked, wondering for the second time tonight why his beer-mug was already empty. He was starting to drink again. Not a good sign.

"It is, believe me," Elias replied with a nod, smiling calmly.

If there weren't those moving gears and wheels visible behind Elias' dark eyes, Frank wouldn't have had any hope of getting Johann out of this alive. But the man facing him wouldn't be here if he hadn't at least an idea how to get their mutual friend out of the situation he was currently in. And if all that Frank could do was to be around and show his face, then he would do exactly that. In the end, Elias was trained to get people out of jail as much as Frank was trained to kill people. Neither could claim to know much about the other's tricks of the trade.

Stifling a hearty yawn, Elias clearly signaled that he was about to retire for the night. Stretching his long limbs, he waved for the waiter.

"I think I'll be off to bed now, Frank, if that is okay with you," he announced, absent-mindedly paying his share of the bill.

"Sure." For a second, Frank wondered what to do with the rest of the evening on his own, watching the polite exchange of pleasantries between Elias and the waiter. Then he decided to do something about the empty mug in front of him before going anywhere else. Sarcastically, he added, "And if you don't mind, then I'll still stay here for a while and get reacquainted with the local customs."

Laughing gently, Elias nodded, slipping into his jacket and taking his hat. Gathering up his umbrella and the briefcase he had brought with him, he tipped his hat in silent goodbye and left the pub, the heavy cigarette-smoke curling behind him like the best London fog.

For a split second, there was this nagging thought on the edge of Frank's mind that maybe Elias didn't know what he was going to do after all. That he was just playing for time and hoping he would have a brilliant idea before it was too late.

But as swiftly as the thought had come, Frank banished it again. He mustn't stop believing in his cause; in their cause. He had risked so much to help Johann, even if only by showing his support for him. There just had to be a chance.

With a certain, grim determination, Frank stood up from the corner bench he had been sitting on, walking over to the bar with the beer-mug and his coaster in his hand. What better way was there to stop thinking unwanted thoughts than to get senselessly drunk?

"*Noch eins!*" he ordered as soon as the lad behind the counter had noticed him, waving his coaster, trying to act as much like a local as he could.

With the constant buzz of the foreign language around him, bit by bit he felt his thoughts happening more and more in German, and more and more of the words he had thought long forgotten returned to him.

Turning around, his elbows casually resting on the counter, Frank let his eyes wander around the place. Dark and narrow, it seemed, filled with people and smoke and chatter. Dark wooden beams decorated with pewter plates or the occasional deer-head. Walls that had gone yellow with age, covered with everything from enamel beer ads to a large, hand-written cardboard sign with clumsy translations of the menu's most important parts into English, French and Russian, respectively.

As the place was regularly frequented by various foreigners that had come here for the trials, the sign made perfect sense, but it still struck Frank as odd. Would that be the future of this country? Ruled for the rest of eternity by several countries that didn't even speak the local population's language? Or would the victorious forces be able to sort out the internal disagreements and lead this broken country back into independence and a hopefully peaceful future?

"*Entschuldigung!*" A boy's firm and slightly reproachful voice kicked him out of his once again brooding mood. "*Ihr Bier...*"

It was the youngster behind the bar, reminding Frank that even if he didn't want to acknowledge the swift service, he wasn't supposed to let his beer get stale. Smiling, he took his drink with an appropriately acknowledging nod. Instead of paying, he handed him his coaster, where the boy merely added another deft stroke of his pencil before handing the coaster back to Frank.

"*Danke*," he said, feeling slightly proud at the fact that he was obviously considered sufficiently local and trustworthy not to have to pay each beer, but to gather them as marks on his coaster and pay them in full before he left. Frank was just about to turn back around as that certain itch on his neck told him that he was being watched.

Taking a deep breath, Frank hoped it wouldn't be the GI's he had met the night before. Those really were the last guys he wanted to see right now. And slightly intoxicated as he already was, he couldn't guarantee that they would only get wounded this time.

However, as he unobtrusively turned around to see who was staring at him, Frank only found another young man standing at the bar next to him, turning away as soon as Frank returned his look.

"*Kennen wir uns?*" he asked, trying not to sound as misanthropic as he currently felt and failing miserably.

"*Ich nicht — sprechen...*" the other man stammered, "I don't speak German. At least not very well."

Smiling despite himself at the young man's obvious unease, Frank wondered where he had seen him before. He never forgot a face he had seen, and this was one of them. Wavy brown hair, cute brown eyes, a slight build and a little lanky, civilian clothes...

"Aren't you Jackson's aide?" Frank asked. "I remember seeing you in court."

"You... saw me?" the young man replied in genuine surprise, actually blushing to the tip of his ears. "I..."

"What? Are you supposed to be invisible?"

"I... no." Shrugging, the young man tried for an insecure smile. "It's just — normally, everybody treats me as if I were."

"Well," Frank replied with a grave nod and a cheeky smirk, "that's a talent that shouldn't be underestimated."

Apparently not really convinced, the aide stood there for a moment, taking a sip of his own beer for lack of a better idea. Then, as if trying to get over with it, he stretched out his hand, introducing himself.

"Sorry. I am Benedict de Havilland, of the New York de Havillands. That is, Benny for all but Mr. Jackson."

Smiling, Frank took the offered hand.

"Frank."

"Captain Frank Hawthorne, yes." Now smiling himself, Benedict added, "I saw you in court."

Despite his former decision to get thoroughly drunk tonight, Frank felt like it would be a good idea to talk a little longer with the guy. After all, he was aide to their biggest current problem, and insecure and lost as Benny seemed, he would surely open up once he felt treated like a visible person for a change.

"What about having our beer together?" Frank suggested, pointing at the table in the corner he had just come from. "I wouldn't mind some company."

"Wouldn't-" Benedict started, but abruptly cut himself short. Pausing, he then explained. "I don't want to get you into trouble with von Biehn's lawyer. After all, we're supposed to be enemies."

No, we're supposed to be on the same side, Frank almost snapped back. We are supposed to be the good guys in this game. But he didn't voice his thoughts, it was neither the place nor the situation for something as philosophical as that. And anyway, something was fishy with the boy, Frank was sure of that. He couldn't really put his finger on it, but he just felt... wrong. Benedict gave him the impression that he didn't feel too comfortable with the whole situation, and that usually was a very bad sign.

"Don't worry," Frank replied, already gently pushing Benedict towards the table. "I've got as much as no idea whatsoever of judicial stuff. You could probably tell me everything about your side of the case and I wouldn't understand much more than the fact that you're working for the prosecution."

"Maybe you're right," Benny replied tersely. Sitting down on the bench, he took a moment to stare at the ornate wrought-iron monstrosity in the middle of the table that was supposed to be an ashtray in appalled wonder.

Giving a soft sigh, he turned his attention back to his beer-mug, taking a deep draught.

Benny seemed genuinely nice, Frank admitted to himself, but why was he acting so uncomfortable? Who was forcing him to do something he did not want to?

"Jackson sent you here to spy on me, didn't he?" Frank asked, mostly guessing by his gut instinct. But the renewed deep blush on Benedict told him that he had hit the bull's eye on first attempt. "He did."

"Yes." The answer was hardly audible, and Benedict looked so miserable that Frank almost felt pity for the boy. Almost.

But then suddenly, Benedict flustered with outrage that was more amusing than anything else.

"What is it that makes the few people who actually see me able to look right into my thoughts?"

"I don't know." Frank replied with a lopsided grin. "Maybe it's that you're a good person. And good people just don't lie."

Sighing in overly dramatic despair, Benny nodded, staring into his beer-mug.

"I'll never make a good lawyer."

Which was a statement Frank preferred not to comment on. Instead, he took a deep draught of his beer himself, setting the mug down with an audible bang.

"I am a dangerous killer," he pointed out, smirking at Benny's suddenly worried expression. "And I really have no idea of court proceedings or what I am doing here exactly."

Still Benny stared at him, slightly hunched over his beer-mug, apparently waiting for a reason to bolt and run. But with a soft smile, Frank asked, "Now that we have properly introduced ourselves, can we go on with having a nice evening anyway?"

"So you're not sending me away?" Benny asked, immediately grimacing at his own question.

"No, why should I?" Gesturing with his beer, Frank explained, "We know who we are, and why we are here. So what's keeping us from getting drunk together?"

"I... I don't know." Slowly, Benedict seemed to relax at the fact that his "cover" didn't even last a second. "Probably nothing."

Now finally smiling in a way that Frank didn't think was forced, Benny finished what was left of his beer, setting the gray mug down with another thud. Shaking his head, he laughed softly.

"I don't think Mr. Jackson had meant to order me to get pissed, but I don't think he'll be able to complain either." Turning serious, he added with a voice that hinted at a bone-weary emotional exhaustion, "Truce?"

"Truce," Frank replied instantly, not really worried about giving away too much to this boy. At least, not while drinking beer.

As if to seal their treaty, he raised his mug as well, finishing his portion in one long draught. Shuddering as the drink's chill spread through his body, he placed down his mug with a thud answering Benny's earlier one.

For one moment, both men exchanged a silent glance, somewhere between sizing up and curiosity. Then Benedict smiled cheekily and waved for a passing waiter.

"*Noch zwei Bier,*" he ordered with a rather heavy accent, apparently having learned the phrase phonetically. "Two more beer," he had said, and there was little Frank could add to that, except maybe one thing.

"*Für mich bitte auch zwei!*" he called at the waiter. For me, two as well.

It took Benedict a delightful three seconds to piece together what Frank had just said, but then he burst into uproarious laughter. Nodding with tears in his eyes, he confirmed the order, shaking his head at Frank.

"You act like you feel at home here, you know that?" Benny asked as he had calmed down sufficiently. Looking curious now, he inquired. "Do you?"

Faced with this somewhat unexpected question, Frank realized that he didn't have an instant answer. Maybe, he wondered, this evening wouldn't be as dull as he had feared.

***

August 1943, Spreewald, von Biehn Manor

"Well then," Frank announced as he finished his last glass of wine, "I think I'll hobble back to my shed now."

Dinner had been delightful, to say the least.

Apart from a few moments where it seemed neither Frank nor Johann were sure how to circumvent some unpleasant subjects other than by not speaking at all, they had chatted most animatedly. The food had been surprisingly good, as well as the wine. The lovely sunset had added an almost surreal touch to this already rather hard-to-believe moment, followed by a star-studded sky and a bright crescent moon. They had talked about traveling the world, about food and theater and rugby and Russian poetry, God and the world and everything in between. Frank had to admit that von Biehn's company was delightful, charming and just that little bit irritating that told him it would take many years before they would ever grow bored.

Despite his announced intention, von Biehn had so far abstained from making any attempt at openly seducing Frank; nor had he given the impression that he expected Frank to show that certain kind of "gratitude." If at all, it had been Frank who was acting more interested, but Johann had ignored any offer to turn the talk to more sensual matters.

So after a long while of sitting in the warm summer night, with the gramophone softly scratching classical music and the occasional French chanson in the background, Frank had decided that this was leading nowhere and he could just as well go to bed and get a good night of sleep. Somehow, he almost felt a little disappointed.

"If you don't mind," von Biehn suggested in a slightly slurred voice, sounding more tired than he looked, "I have prepared one of the guest rooms for you here in the manor." With an almost boyish grin, he added, "No need for the shed now, you see?"

It didn't take Frank long to decide. The shed was nice, and one could really sleep well on that recliner. But it still was not a real bed, so he replied with a nod, "Sure, thank you."

Once again, an odd silence followed, with both men only watching each other in the low candlelight. Von Biehn did look good, Frank decided, in a neat, manly way. Given that he wasn't too sure if there would come another opportunity in his life for a good romp, Frank was more than reluctant to let this one pass by.

But in the end, it was Johann who made the decision.

"The guest room is at the end of the corridor, to the right." Folding his napkin, von Biehn put it down onto the table and stood up, gesturing Frank to wait. "I'll fetch you a cane. That should be better for you."

Silently, he left the balcony, only to return a moment later with a black walking cane, complete with a silver handle the shape of an eagle's head.

"Here," he said as he offered it to Frank, his smile bittersweet.

Frank took the offered cane, returning Johann's enigmatic smile. "Is this also your grandmother's?" he asked as he stood up, taking great care to look appropriately challenged with the task.

75

"No, it's mine," von Biehn replied, apparently bemused with the image of his late grandmother hobbling around with a cane. "For the rare occasions I go to the opera in something other than my uniform."

Frank could almost see Johann in black tails, complete with top hat, bow tie and cane stepping out of a limousine in front of the Berlin opera, so debonair and handsome. He'd look stunning.

Unfortunately, there was also the image of von Biehn leaving the same car on the same occasion, only wearing his Wehrmacht uniform instead. Indeed just as striking, but in a completely different context.

With a soft sigh, Frank nodded, hobbling towards the balcony's door leading back inside into the study.

"Good night, Johann," he said, trying hard not to show how irritated he felt with the course the evening had taken. "And thanks for the dinner, it was very nice."

"You are welcome," Johann replied, following each of Frank's steps as if he were genuinely worried he might fall. But he didn't support him either, apparently well aware that Frank wouldn't have appreciated the assistance.

If that man would only stop acting so... gallant, Frank thought once again. *Why did such a decent guy have to end up so entangled on the very worst side of the war?*

Right then, Frank had to cross the tiny step that led from the balcony back into the study. Caught up in his thoughts as he was, he kept leaning on the cane, and naturally it slipped away under his weight on the glistening, waxed parquetry of the study.

Instantly, Johann was at his side, supporting him, holding him. Frank could see him biting down a smile at his guest's obvious stubbornness.

Frank had to bite down a curse himself, angry at his clumsiness and his condition. And angry at the fact that it now looked as if he was trying to seduce von Biehn.

Though, on second thought, it wasn't all bad. Johann's arms still held him tightly, his chest firm and warm and so inviting to lean against for a moment.

"*Alles in Ordnung, Süßer?*" von Biehn asked gently, not loosening his embrace at all. Is everything all right, he had asked, making Frank nod.

Still reluctant to leave Johann's embrace, Frank wondered why on earth he was trying so hard not to end up in Johann's bed. It would increase his chances for survival and probably be a good fuck as well. And von Biehn smelled pretty damn good, too, he noticed, of all things.

"Breakfast will be tomorrow morning at eight," Johann continued, smiling at Frank's hesitation to leave his arms.

His face was so close to Frank's ear that he could feel the warm breath on his skin, and it was an unexpectedly pleasant sensation. "On the balcony, it'll be warm enough by then."

"Yes," Frank replied, straightening up but still making no effort to move away. In contrary, he snaked an arm of his own around von Biehn's waist ever so chastely and waited for a reaction.

"Down the hall, right hand opposite the bathroom," Johann repeated his directions for Frank's bedroom, his voice brimming with amusement. "Your room."

"Yes," Frank repeated, now turning to face Johann. Feeling a bit silly but still rather good, he asked in a voice that was both mocking and sultry at the same time. "And yours?"

Von Biehn blinked in surprise before the dirtiest smirk Frank had so far seen appeared on his face. He hesitated a moment, several unreadable expressions rushing across his face before he finally answered.

"It's on this floor as well. Fancy a look?"

Chapter 6
Coupling

September 1946, downtown Nuremberg

Laughing, Frank and Benedict walked along the cobblestone road. It was in the middle of the night, much later than either of them had actually planned to be out. But the time they had spent in the pub together had been a carefree break from the dreadfully slow moving proceedings at court for Frank. And judging by his companion's slightly intoxicated mood, it had been a nice evening for Benedict as well.

Frank had thought twice about spending this evening together with Benedict at the pub. After all, he was the personal aide to a man who was intent on getting Johann executed. On the other hand, Benny seemed like genuinely nice company, and a most welcome change to the constant double-edged games Frank's world seemed to be made of currently.

So they had had several beers together, telling stories of the war, or at least Frank telling stories and Benedict listening. He had never realized how much his operations during the war sounded hard to believe. If he hadn't been there himself, he would have wondered if such stories could contain even a single grain of truth. Seriously, jumping out of planes at night into enemy territory to single-handedly kill off one of them! It sounded more like the stuff pulp novels were made of, not a soldier's life.

Except that he had been there, and lived the life that now seemed so unreal even to him.

Not that any of this mattered any longer, Frank thought to himself. He had risked close to everything by coming to Germany, and what remained of his life back home would be decided with the outcome of Johann's trial.

Better not to waste too much thought on tomorrow, he reminded himself.

Smiling at the thought, he turned his attention back to the young man at his side. Benedict gave him a slightly drunken smile, telling him he was pleasantly intoxicated. He looked like he had had a splendid evening and was thoroughly looking forward to his bed now.

Which was where they were going, actually. After having decided that they had had enough beer, they had left the pub together. Once outside on the road, they had noticed that they shared a good part of the way, and somewhere along the way, Frank had decided that he would walk the youngster home.

The war was over, sure. But even despite that and everything they had done to free the German population, Nuremberg at night still was only a bit better than enemy territory. And after the encounter Frank had had the night before with his own people, he trusted the silent darkness even less than usual.

"So what are you going to tell Jackson tomorrow morning?" Frank asked, smiling at Benedict's answering groan.

"Don't ask me about that," he replied, rolling his eyes. "I obviously can't lie, so I might as well tell the truth."

"And that would be...?"

This time, Benny grinned at the question.

"I'll tell him that we met in the bar, that we chatted the whole night long and had a few beers too many." Hesitantly, he bit his lower lip, adding, "That we became friends."

"Sounds good to me," Frank agreed with a grin, answering the younger man's unspoken question. "Maybe he'll be too busy to ask for details."

This Benedict definitely was a complete failure as a lawyer, Frank silently determined. He was carrying his heart on his sleeve to a degree that was plain deadly for that profession. But apart from that, he was an utterly decent chap, and a pretty one too, with his romantic hair and the long lashes. He should get himself a decent girl and a decent job, and everything would be fine.

Casting a glance at the young man walking next to him, Frank had to fight hard to keep down a dirty grin. *Now look at me*, he thought vaguely amused, *all I need is a handsome boy with an honest smile and I feel happy again.*

Not that he had any intention of hitting on Benny, not even remotely so. It would only be trouble for the boy, and definitely improper since he was here for the man Frank had decided was his one true love. But the thought of tumbling in the sheets with him was refreshing, nice, and so perfectly suited to distract from the gloom he had been wallowing in of late.

It was an image to hold on to, Frank thought, and something to keep his spirits up in the dark of the night, when thinking of Johann would only entrench him further in futile worries.

"Well, here we are." Benedict suddenly said, and it took Frank a while to understand that they had reached the place where Benny had rented his room. "Thanks for the company."

It was a dark alleyway without working street lights yet, the only light coming from the crossing main road's illumination. Even though this part of town had not been hit by the bombings, the houses still bore the pockmarks of some gunfight and many of the windows were merely nailed shut with wooden planks. But the corners were free from rubble, and everywhere there were signs of people working hard to repair their property.

Life always goes on, Frank thought with certain amazement, *at least for those who survive.*

Suddenly remembering Benedict, who already had walked up the few steps towards the house's entrance, he flicked on his smile again, surprising himself with his beaming mood.

"Sure," he said cheerfully. "Anytime. Do you have a day off? We could go have another beer, then."

Such sparkling eyes, such a pretty nose... Grinning inwardly at the realization that he had a serious but delightfully harmless crush on the boy, Frank found that he indeed was looking forward to meeting him again. And that he was unspeakably grateful to Benedict for giving him something else to think of.

"Not really, but we have days when we're supposed to dawdle off the over-hours." Grimacing, Benny added, "Not that anybody actually makes use of it, nor that we ever would be able to break even. But I think no one could complain when I took leave for say, half a day, so I could go out the night before."

"Sounds great."

"What about Wednesday evening?" Benny suggested, his face lighting up when Frank nodded.

"Sure, really looking forward to it." His own smile softening a little, he said, "See you again on Wednesday. Bye, then!"

And acting completely out of instinct, Frank stepped up the stairs and hugged Benny fiercely, glad to feel anything but depressed. Not waiting for any reaction, he let go of the boy immediately again, smiled and started to walk away.

When he turned around after a few steps, he could see Benedict still standing there as if struck by lightning. Grinning, Frank waved at the other man, calling out, "'Til Wednesday!"

Still Benny didn't react, but Frank didn't really care. With a last look at Benny, Frank walked out of the alley, feeling slightly intoxicated and in a good mood for the second time this day already.

***

What Frank didn't see, though, was that Benedict remained standing in the dark doorway for quite a while, his keys all but forgotten in his hand, his face stunned but rather pleasantly so.

Slowly, he reached for his cheek, where only moments ago he had felt the fleeting touch of Frank's scratchy skin against his own. With a deep, wistful sigh, Benedict leaned back against the doorway, smiling and shaking his head at the same time.

"If only..." Benedict murmured dazedly, closing his eyes for a second and then forcing himself to sober up again.

Determined, he took the keys and unlocked the door, finding the keyhole rather by habit than by sight. But opening the door, he suddenly hesitated, looking down the alley where Frank had disappeared around the corner.

"If only?" he whispered again, this time though with more question than wish in his voice. Chewing his lower lip, he stared into the night, thinking rapidly, his whole posture frozen in the moment. Then, suddenly, his face went slack with surprise as some parts in his mind suddenly connected.

"Oh my God," he whispered into the night. "They're a couple!"

***

August 1943, Spreewald, von Biehn manor
"So, how do you like it?" von Biehn asked as he blew out the match he had used to light a lamp on the night-stand. When Frank didn't reply, he added with a cheeky smirk, "The bedroom, *Süßer*, only the bedroom."

Laughing softly with relief, Frank nodded. He really wouldn't have known how to answer that question otherwise. So he took his time looking around while his host lit some more candles. The whole room was dominated by the huge canopied bed; whitewashed wood and fine white curtains.

"It's very...clean," Frank truthfully voiced his first impression, earning a low chuckle from Johann. "And a very big bed for an unmarried man."

At that, von Biehn looked at his own bed with an expression as if he was seeing it the first time. "Not really," he replied evenly with a shrug, "I live unmarried, not celibate."

"Do you often show your bedroom to guests?" Frank continued his playful questions, walking around as silently as his damaged ankle and the cane allowed.

"Not as often as I would like to," von Biehn answered, watching Frank intently. "And never before to a guest as exclusive as you are."

"Exclusive, huh?" Frank smirked at the phrase, turning his attention back to von Biehn. "And now?"

Instead of an answer, Johann walked up to Frank with a soft smile, taking the cane out of his hands.

"You won't need that again, tonight, *Süßer*," he said and carelessly discarded it into a corner of the room. "If need be, I can still carry you a few steps."

Almost a bit hesitant, Johann reached out with his hand, setting it against Frank's chest in a cautious gesture. His eyes were firmly locked with the other man, and he seemed to wait for some kind of rejection that never came. Finally, von Biehn smiled, a gentle and even a little shy gesture, and closed the remaining distance between them with a single step.

Now standing right in front of each other, their hips touching, Frank realized for the first time that they were about the same height and that he could look into the other man's eyes straight in front of him.

A first wave of arousal washed through his body, warm and tingling and welcome. Without another word, Frank snaked one arm around Johann's waist, while his other hand firmly grabbed the man's neck. He could feel how much Johann reveled in the sensation of his tight embrace, could smell him underneath his expensive aftershave and the wine and the cigarettes in a cloud of man and warmth and desire.

Bending von Biehn's head just a little, Frank placed a kiss on the other man's lips; probing at first, a little insecure and curious. But it took only a few heartbeats for Johann to abandon all pretense of shyness. Frank found his kiss returned first carefully, then longingly, and in the end with nothing but deep and relaxed passion.

When they finally separated, Frank laughed softly.

"Now that wasn't shy," he commented on the other man's reaction, sensually licking his own lips.

"Just trying to keep up with my guest's advances," von Biehn replied cheekily, tilting his head back to get a better view of Frank.

His hands started inching beneath Frank's sweater. Still looking straight into Frank's eyes, Johann's hands explored the skin underneath, his face twitching with delight, his eyes sparkling. Where Frank's chest wasn't wrapped up in bandages, he could feel von Biehn's fingers trace lines along his smooth skin, his lean muscle, and down along the sparse hair forming a trail down into his pants.

With a widening grin, Johann lifted the sweater above his "prisoner's" head, halting when Frank cursed softly as his attempt to help reminded him that the wounds weren't fully healed yet. More careful now, Frank got rid of it in his own time, and he could almost feel Johann's eyes roaming all over his body in the meanwhile.

When Frank dropped the sweater to the ground and looked up to his host again, he found von Biehn smiling, his eyes shining with what looked like genuine awe. Without a word, Johann curled a finger in the waistband of Frank's trousers, pulling them into another close embrace. With a dreamy expression, he let the fingers of his free hand trail down Frank's muscled chest, licking his lips. Only when his fingertips reached the scar that a Moroccan camel-trader's scimitar had left just above Frank's last rib on the right, he hesitated for a moment.

He continued his caress until he reached Frank's belly, slipping right into his pants, cupping Frank's cock with his hand. The touch made him grow hard almost instantly, and Frank could see how much Johann enjoyed what was happening in his hand. Frank had never made love to anyone he could read as easily as Johann, and he found himself immensely turned on by the thought.

"So, before we take this any further," Johann asked leisurely while continuing to teasingly massage Frank's dick, "You have been with a man before?"

With his attention mostly occupied in his pants, Frank only nodded. It wasn't his most in-depth field of experience, but he wasn't untouched either. No pun intended.

"On the receiving end?" Johann continued both his questions and caresses, sounding rather surprised at the first answer already.

This time, Frank hesitated a moment longer before he could answer. For one, the attention von Biehn gave his dick was too pleasing to be ignored, and second, Johann's question brought up a subject he had until now foolishly managed to ignore. Of course Johann hadn't started all this to get thoroughly sodomized himself. He just didn't strike Frank as a man who'd happily lie down to be a mewling recipient of lust.

But neither could Frank see himself in such a position, at least not tonight, not after what had happened that time in the prison of Algiers... With a blink, Frank forced the unpleasant memories back into the dark corner of his mind he had exiled them to.

"No," he replied flatly, if not perfectly truthful.

But Johann only chuckled softly.

"Thought so..." he murmured, sounding as if the feel of Frank's cock hot and hard in his hand was taking up most of his concentration. "Well, we won't let this detail spoil our evening, will we?"

Not that Frank had any real idea of what Johann meant, but it sounded like a good thing, actually. So he nodded his agreement, only to be surprised when Johann suddenly took his hand away.

"Come," von Biehn urged seductively, his voice carrying a stunning allure in Frank's ears despite its tongue-in-cheek tone. Or maybe even exactly because of it. "Let's get a little more comfortable, *Süßer.*"

With gentle insistence, Johann pushed Frank towards the bed, making him sit down on the edge.

At the rustling sound of the starched linen covers, Frank had to smile despite himself, his fingers running across the cool fabric with subtle amusement. *This was so Johann*, he thought, *impeccable and old-fashioned to the point of caricature.* Yet, Johann was real, everything around here was real, only the war and everything else connected to it felt so surreal and far away.

Submitting to the rare feeling of security that spread inside of him, Frank leaned back until his head sank into the thick pillows. Above him, the bed's white canopy formed a sky of dancing gold and cream shadows in the light of the candles, and there was a memory of lavender hanging in the air. When Johann in all earnest knelt down and started taking off Frank's shoes, he couldn't help but chuckle at the image.

"What are you doing there?" he asked, raising his head to look down his chest and rather impressively bulging crotch.

At first, von Biehn only smiled in response, but then he said calmly, "I'm just trying to make you feel comfortable."

"You'll make me fall asleep," Frank mocked gently, pulling his legs up onto the bed with all due respect to his various damages.

"Can't let that happen," Johann stated matter-of-factly, and slipped out of his own shoes while simultaneously beginning to unbutton his shirt. Licking his lips at the admittedly pleasant sight, Frank watched while the other man climbed onto the bed as well, straddling himself across Frank's hips with promising agility. "I'll have to provide some entertainment, then, *ne c'est pas?*"

Slowly Johann continued taking off his shirt in all detail, giving Frank such a perfect view that it was quite obvious he was putting in some reasonable effort to make it look natural. Finally flinging the thin cloth away, von Biehn looked down with such a horny and delighted expression that it made Frank grin in return.

"Gods," Johann whispered huskily, again one of his hands trailing down the other man's chest. "You're so beautiful... Are you sure you aren't an angel?"

"Absolutely."

The sentiment, as sweet as it was, only caused a bitter laugh in Frank. *If anything at all,* he added silently, *I'm an angel of death.*

Johann bit his lower lip, as if focusing not to miss a single second of this all.

He's really struck with me, Frank suddenly realized. *He's not faking any of this.*

As if hearing Frank's silent thoughts, von Biehn suddenly smiled, a warm and slightly melancholic expression that made Frank wonder if Johann maybe wasn't a little too complex to simply fall head-over-heels for the next best enemy killer who dropped into his yard.

With a tiny kiss on Frank's lips, Johann leaned to the side and started rummaging in his nightstand's drawer. Returning with a small vial of scented oil, he smirked at Frank.

"Here," he said while handing the flask to Frank. "You open that blasted thing, and I'll take care of these annoying pants..."

Indeed, "that blasted thing" was rather difficult to open, and Frank really had other things on his mind than concentrating on a tiny cork slippery with oil. Things like Graf Oberst Johann von Biehn busy getting him out of his pants, like him almost reverentially stroking the exposed dick and laughing with the shivers it caused in Frank.

Swiftly and somehow discreetly, Johann managed to get out of his own remaining clothes as well, only to settle back on Frank's lap immediately. For a long moment, Johann seemed unable to think of anything else but the other man's hot dick between his legs, but then returned his concentration to the matters at hand with a visible effort.

Frank still hadn't managed to open the vial, and admittedly, he hadn't paid much attention. So Johann took it from his hands, opening the reluctant cork with his teeth. Generously oiling his hands, he used one to continue massaging Frank's throbbing cock while the other one wandered to his own rear to prepare himself, as far as Frank could see.

This rather unexpected turn of events made Frank quirk a pleasantly surprised eyebrow, at least as much as his rather excited state allowed him any other expression than a breathless moan.

With malicious glee, Johann grinned at the obvious effect he was having on Frank. For a few moments, he continued stroking the length of the other man's cock, only to halt when Frank was already close to coming. Frank wasn't sure if he was grateful for the pause or not, his almost painfully hard cock throbbing with need.

"Been a long time for you, huh?" Johann asked, raising an eyebrow with slightly amused sympathy.

And he was right, Frank thought, *once again.* Lying in a Nazi garden shed with some mean bruises, a concussion and a sprained ankle didn't exactly inspire solo adventures, and the last time for him before he had jumped out of that plane... Well, enough to say it really had been a long time. So he nodded with a sheepish grin, wriggling with his eyebrows while making his cock bob up and down simultaneously.

Von Biehn's wide grin definitely gained an even sleazier edge.

"I like hungry soldiers," he said in a low growl, carefully placing himself above Frank's dick. "They don't last long, but many times..."

Johann then lowered himself slowly, taking in Frank's dick with a low gasp of lust. Biting his knuckles with the intensity of the sensation, Johann seemed completely absorbed until he had fully impaled himself, a fine sheen of sweat beginning to cover his forehead.

This was all moving so fast for Frank, almost too fast, in a way. But then again, feeling his dick buried deeply inside the other man was the only thing he craved right now. That and to fuck him hard, to thrust his hard flesh into Johann's ass and come with all the explosive force of the passion he had dammed up until now.

Most pleasantly, Johann seemed to share his thoughts.

"Let's make the first one fast," he whispered urgently, twitching with hardly suppressed desire himself. "Come as soon as you can, as hard as you can. I need it..."

Once again not waiting for a reply from Frank, Johann started to move on Frank's dick, taking his length with an appetite that bordered on gluttony. All the while, he kept his eyes open, staring at Frank as if it would be a crime to miss any bit of his passion.

And apart from a stunned gasp, there was nothing Frank could say. Johann had saddled him with an expertise he had never expected to see this side of a brothel, riding him hard and wild and tight and completely focused on making Frank come as fast as possible.

"Oh ... my - " was about everything Frank was able to get out before he felt himself rapidly approach his climax, mercilessly pushed over the threshold by Johann's efficient motions. Grabbing Johann by his waist, Frank gasped with his eyes wide open as he felt himself collapse around the sensation of his throbbing cock, deeply buried inside of Johann, all his being whisked away in a singular wave of lust as intense and uncompromising as he had never before experienced.

Like an explosion, he felt himself come deep inside Johann, pumping hot and hard into him, releasing a tension that was almost more than merely sexual. Staring at the other man with a stammering sound on his lips, Frank for a long, long moment was hardly able to breathe, let alone think independently. Pretending that he was still wounded and hardly able to move was about the last thing Frank cared about right now.

This had been too swift, too much what he wanted, too surprising for him to comprehend properly. His body shivering, his hands hardly able to hold on to Johann's sides, he bucked up jerkily until the waves of almost painful pleasure subsided.

"Why..." he gasped breathlessly, surprising himself with how brittle his voice sounded. "Why'd you do this?"

Still sweating slightly, Johann only managed a low chuckle. Taking his time to regain his composure, he finally managed to reply with utter conviction. "'Cause I wanted to. Because I wanted to see those wonderful eyes of yours burning with passion, wide and out of focus when you come." Managing a shaky grin, he added, "Don't think I've done that for you, American, this one was pure selfishness."

At the tell-tale shudder that wrecked Johann right then, Frank could tell he had seriously meant what he had said. What a hot thought, to have a lover who took his pleasure from giving pleasure to him, Frank mused. What a gift.

Slowly, Johann started to move his hips again, gently rekindling the fire in Frank that he had so expertly doused before.

"Ready for a second course?" von Biehn asked under his breath, grinning with his own indecency, and Frank found himself most willing to oblige. Actually, it would be his pleasure absolutely.

"Only under one condition," he commented though, taking Johann's rock-hard dick into his own hands, "that you have your first course as well."

Laughing at the reprise, von Biehn nodded, leaning back to offer Frank the best access to his cock possible.

"I'm all yours," he replied, officially initiating what Frank would come to remember as the longest fuck in his whole life.

Chapter 7
The Morning After

September 1946, Nuremberg, office of Chief Prosecutor Jackson

"So, I heard you spent the evening with Captain Hawthorne?" Jackson asked out of the blue as Benedict brought him his morning coffee.

That meant it was half past six in the morning and Benedict was hardly able to keep his eyes open. Not only had he spent the evening with Frank indeed, their farewell had also left Benedict with certain conclusions about the relationship between the American and Oberst von Biehn. Certain rather personal conclusions; and Benedict had found it hard to sleep in what little remained of his night, tossing and turning and wondering how to deal with his suspicion.

But right now there were Jackson's narrow eyes drilling holes in Benedict's head, and he had to react somehow at least. So he nodded to his employer, praying that with the respectable hangover he had, he wouldn't mess up things too badly.

"And?" Jackson asked impatiently, cooling down his coffee to a drinkable temperature with some water from a jug left over from the other day. "Benedict, did you get anything useful out of this utterly unwieldy witness?"

"I..." Benedict began nervously, torn between showing off his conclusions and fearing that Jackson would tear him apart as his conclusions were based on nothing but a hug and probably wishful thinking on his own part. "I don't know..."

Obviously unsurprised, Jackson gave a contemptuous snort and gulped down his coffee in a single draught. Then he turned his attention back to Benedict, snapping, "So you learned at least something." As Benedict still didn't say anything, he added with growing annoyance, "I'm waiting, Benedict."

But apart from the fact that his suspicion would never be based on sufficient fact in Jackson's eyes, there was another problem nagging on Benedict's mind: He liked Hawthorne. He didn't want to betray the first man who had treated him like a decent person in years, and surely that was what Jackson wanted of him.

Of course, it would only do harm if his suspicion was true, but in that case the prosecution would be able to annihilate von Biehn's already threadbare defense, surely seeing that the Oberst was executed. That way, Benedict would have had a direct hand in killing Hawthorne's lover, and that was about the last thing he wanted to do.

Oh, admittedly, there had been moments when Benedict had lain awake last night, wondering if there maybe was a chance for himself as Frank would surely need some consolation after seeing von Biehn condemned to death. But that thought was inappropriate in so many ways he definitely didn't want to think about it any longer.

Despite efforts not to, Benedict felt himself blush up to his ears, once again deeply embarrassed that he was able to harbor such low intentions.

At his desk, Jackson furrowed his brow even further.

"Benedict..." he all but growled. "We both know you can't hide shit from anybody, and surely not from me. So what the hell happened last night?"

Blushing even deeper with the fact that he hadn't been able to hide his embarrassment, with his own sinful intentions and last but not least with the fact that he felt kind of disappointed that indeed nothing had happened last night, Benedict shook his head.

Oh Lord, he prayed silently, hoping that for once he would find a way out of the mess he had gotten himself into, *why me?*

***

August 1943, Spreewald, von Biehn Manor

It was still early in the morning when Frank woke up, and judging by the rather pleasant aches in various private parts of his body, he hadn't spent much of the night sleeping. Next to him, Johann was still sleeping peacefully with a light wheeze, and Frank was quite happy about it. Johann's face was relaxed, only a hint of worry remaining on his features.

If only things were a little different, Frank wondered wistfully. This was a man he could get used to waking up next to.

He got out of the bed silently and left the room, grabbing the first vaguely suitable piece of clothing he could make out in what little light the heavy curtains let in. Only when he soundlessly closed the door behind him did Frank realize it was the sable slacks von Biehn had worn last night. Not that either of them had worn much at all most of the night...

At the thought of the night he had spent with Johann, Frank felt a deeply satisfied shiver run down his body. Hell, this had been good. If the situation had been any different, this single night would have made him consider changing his whole life.

There it was again. Being with von Biehn seemed to affect his judgment more than Frank would have thought ever possible.

But unfortunately, things were as they were, and Frank was here on a mission. The sex last night might have shaken the foundations of the earth, several times actually, but it hadn't shaken Frank's determination. Several of the most brilliant Nazi minds would convene here in little more than a week, and it was his duty to take out as many of them as possible, harming the Aryan system as much as possible.

With a sigh, Frank slipped into the trousers he had found, surprised at how cool the place had become after the warm evening yesterday. At least von Biehn's slacks fit him comfortably.

Frank had known that there was no reason other than a shitload of luck that he would survive this mission, and he had gladly accepted it anyway. He was deeply convinced that it had to be done, that it helped in saving a lot of his fellow countrymen, that it helped to end the war and thus would save many innocent lives. His own life counted little in comparison. No good fuck would change any of this. It only made things so much more personal.

Not good, he thought grimly. Not good, but definitely not the worst situation he had been in.

Forcing a brave smile onto his face, Frank started a silent tour of the place. Last evening, he had paid some attention to which rooms might be important and which ones were probably for public use. And with his host still sleeping off the blissful exhaustion of the night, there was no reason for him not to embark on an extended expedition.

Even though it could have hardly been later than six o'clock in the morning, it was light outside already. Birds were singing their little lungs out, and it looked like the promise of another beautiful day in paradise. Smiling, Frank looked out onto the gardens that surrounded the manor, surprised as he saw there were still big patches of mist lingering on the lawns between the trees, the small rivers surrounding the manor's island still completely shrouded in white.

It looked as if nature itself was still snuggled in her bed, lazily dozing until she felt like finally getting up.

Smiling at the thought, Frank continued exploring the manor as silently as he could. Everywhere, he found traces of a long family history taking place here in this building. In one room, there was a huge painting above the chimney, looking as if it had been painted well over a century ago. It depicted an outdoor wedding party, dozens of people strolling through a park, and in the background, he could see the von Biehn manor rise behind the treetops.

What made Frank wonder after a while, though, was the rather obvious absence of any Nazi insignia. No swastika flags or emblems, no Führer portraits, no current medals proudly on display. The only noteworthy item was a set of sculptures in the current "realistic" style on a buffet. But as they depicted a group of quite handsomely muscled shirtless farmers, Frank suspected the reason behind their acquisition had nothing to do with political correctness at all.

Frank's bemused smile only faded when he realized that he had eventually ended up in von Biehn's study.

So this was where he plotted the victorious advance of the superior race, Frank thought with a heavy heart.

Silently, he walked along the tall bookshelves, reading the covers. There were books from all over the world, some of them in languages even Frank with his extensive training didn't know.

Hell, there was even Marx's *Kapital* and a copy of the US Air Force manual, there were economic treatises from Locke to Keynes, travel diaries from various authors about destinations all over the planet. This wasn't simply a private library; this was a reason for immediate execution if it had been in anybody else's hands but von Biehn's. And we weren't necessarily talking Nazi legislation here.

Heaving a deep sigh, Frank settled in the huge leather armchair behind the desk. Good, massive German oak dark with old age, an expensive pen and ink barrel and irritatingly little paper.

Where did he store his documents? Frank felt his trained senses reawaken, scanning the room for possible hidden safes or other compartments. Almost without thinking, he looked underneath the leather writing mat, opened the desk's drawers one by one, checking their contents.

Nothing, not even some scribbles or a batch of old correspondence, even though this definitely was the only room in the house von Biehn could possibly be working in. Annoyed with the constant feeling of von Biehn being a step ahead of him, Frank almost sighed with relief as he found the lowest drawer locked. A quick glance at the lock confirmed that he wouldn't need more than a paperclip to open it. And he had found plenty of those.

Working silently on the lock for a moment, Frank smirked with satisfaction when the lock gave a tell-tale click, telling him he had won at least this tiny struggle. Inside, he could see a large amount of files, each one carefully labeled and secured, hanging in their register. Curious, he scanned the titles, and had just decided that a swift glance at the documents wouldn't do any harm as a soft sound from the door made him freeze.

The bright morning sun was slanting into the room, and he couldn't make out anything in the dark corridor. Outside, the birds were still chirping madly, but apart from that, everything was calm. Only when Frank had almost come to the conclusion that there wasn't anything at the door, another sound broke the silence.

"So, it seems we're back to work again, are we?" von Biehn's voice asked from the doorway, making Frank flinch with anger. How could he have not overheard the other man walking around the place? Was he really getting that sloppy?

Walking into the study, wearing nothing but a pair of boxers, Johann's face was unreadable. At least, he wasn't carrying a gun and didn't look as if he was about to kill Frank right away. If at all, he looked tired, Frank decided.

"Haven't found anything interesting yet?" Johann stated more than he asked, obviously knowing very well that there wasn't anything to be found.

"You knew why I came here," Frank replied flatly, trying to remind his host that there wasn't any real surprise in his actions. "You know what I am."

"I know," von Biehn replied and actually managed the hint of a smile. "I am just a little hurt that you didn't try to straight-out ask me first. But I am not surprised."

Good for you, Frank was briefly tempted to snap back. But the fact that he wasn't talking to some low-level spy made him bite the retort back.

"So," Frank stated, "It's the next morning. I think it's time to talk business."

"Now, is it..." von Biehn didn't seem too thrilled, but he nodded, his face serious.

Calmly, Johann walked across the room, opening the wide door that led out onto the balcony. A wave of crisp morning air washed into the study, making Frank shiver involuntarily.

"I had hoped we would have this discussion after breakfast," Johann explained, returning his attention to Frank. "But as things are, we should get it over with."

He took a few steps towards Frank, making Frank wonder if ever there would come a moment he and Johann would face each other down the barrel of a gun. And if so, would he still be able to pull the trigger as he had done so many times before?

Probably not.

"So you're here because of the meeting, and you're here to kill whoever of importance you can get, yes?"

Frank didn't see any point in answering that question, so he only nodded vaguely, crossing his arms defensively in front of his naked chest.

But Johann apparently hadn't expected a reaction anyway, for he continued, "And what I am asking of you is that you don't."

This last line had been delivered in absolute earnest, and Frank didn't want to believe his ears. Abandon his mission? On what premise? That Johann asked nicely? Or was his host that naïve that he thought Frank had fallen in love with him? It was so ridiculous that for a long moment Frank didn't say a single word, only kept staring at Johann, his jaw slack with disbelief.

But from the outside, another sound intruded into the relative silence of the room: the distinct bubbling noise of a diesel engine, approaching from somewhere in the dissolving mist; already too close by.

For another heartbeat, Frank and Johann remained utterly silent, both apparently hoping the vessel would pass their island. But the engine got throttled down to a soft gargling sound, followed by the low grating of wood on sand.

"I thought you sent all staff away-" Frank pressed out between his teeth, torn between his urge to bolt and run and an involuntary feeling that he had to stay with Johann.

But Johann only shook his head, gesturing to Frank to remain silent. Swiftly, he cast a glance out across the balcony, but still couldn't make out much beyond the trees. Blinking rapidly, he seemed to gather his thoughts for another heartbeat, then turned to Frank.

"Go back into the bedroom, lock the door." His voice was stressed, but surprisingly firm. Not the voice of a man having to hide a man in his home for the first time. "Stay there, I'll get rid of them."

"Them?" Despite Johann's order, Frank didn't leave his place in the armchair. *This was fishy all over. Had Johann called reinforcements as soon as he had his way with Frank?* The thought was hard to believe, but the timing was too convenient to be coincidental.

Johann only shrugged in reply, casting a hurried glance outside, where the crunch of boot-heels on gravel disrupted the otherwise pastoral morning. Realizing that Frank hadn't made a single move yet, Johann urged, "Go!" Still Frank didn't react, so he added, "Please. No local would ever use a motor boat here, so it's some official with little time. Please go now!"

Somewhere in the back of his mind, Frank remembered reading something of motorized crafts being frowned upon in the area, something about shallow waters and fish spawning grounds and whatnot. Nothing he had ever thought could become relevant in his mission. But it was enough to make him trust Johann once again, at least for now. If Johann had called those people, he'd have told them to use a silent approach.

Frank nodded and rose from his chair behind the desk, swiftly leaving the study. But in passing, von Biehn grabbed his arm, holding him there. His green eyes were filled with something between worry and joy, and his voice bore a faint memory of the pleasure they had shared the last night when he whispered, "I never asked you your name, *Süßer*. I was afraid you wouldn't answer." Despite the circumstances, he managed a tiny smile; the kind of smile that gave Frank goose-bumps of joy every time he thought of it.

"But if I... if this all goes to hell now," Johann continued, "I want to know who I have fallen in love with."

There was such sincerity, such genuine feeling in Johann's words that Frank didn't manage to keep up even a trace of professional doubt.

"Frank," he answered just as softly while prying Johann's fingers off his arm. "My name is Frank."

And with the hint of a smile of his own, he rushed out of the room.

This was madness. Complete and utter madness.

But, in a way, quite lovely, actually.

Chapter 8
A Brush with Disaster

September 1946, Nuremberg, Palace of Justice

Frank had once read about King Minos of Crete, who had a palace like a maze. In its heart, legend said, the Minotaur had lived, a man-devouring creature half human, half bull.

He wondered if that legendary palace had been anywhere near as maze-like as the court building on Fürther Street. There were miles of corridors with ceilings as high as the sky, and many-segmented windows reaching tall with views of the inner yards. But it didn't seem to have any exit, or a place where one could find a decent coffee.

It definitely had its share of resident monsters, though.

Smiling softly at the thought, Frank continued his way down the corridor. He had spent almost all morning in the courtroom, following the proceedings of Johann's trial as one of the few permitted spectators who weren't journalists. And all morning, there had been the annoyingly distracting scent of real coffee hanging in the air.

And now during lunch break, Frank had decided to find out where that scent had been coming from; though it definitely proved much more difficult than he had expected. Despite their superior supplies, real coffee was a rather rare commodity even among the victorious allied forces, and nothing those who had some liked to talk about.

But his nose had always been rather reliable, so finally Frank ended up in a small kitchen somewhere among the apparent miles of conference rooms. And somehow, he wasn't too surprised when he found a young man there, brown hair hanging into his boyish face, clutching a jar of coffee with a look that bordered on guilty.

"Benedict," he greeted the chief persecutor's aide with a wide smile. Leaning against the door frame, Frank crossed his arms in front of his chest, asking, "Feeling fine again, I hope?"

"Captain Hawthorne..." Benedict replied somewhat stumbling, his eyes darting everywhere but looking at the unexpected visitor.

"Captain Hawthorne? I thought it was Frank already the other night."

"I... of course. Sorry." Gesturing nervously, Benedict tried for a smile as well. "How'd you find me?"

"By accident." Benedict's confused look was so cute Frank had to chuckle. "I was looking for coffee in this dreadful maze, and it was my nose that led me here," Frank explained. "I should have known Jackson had some of the real stuff in his private coffers."

"At least making coffee is a task he trusts me with," Benedict complained softly, self-consciously brushing a strand of hair out of his face.

Slowly, there was some sense of alarm waking in Frank. There was something odd in the young man's behavior, something like a bad conscience, something he was desperately trying to hide.

"What's wrong, Benny?" he asked sternly, hoping that there was already enough trust between them. "You're hiding something."

"Nothing," Benedict almost snapped back, much too swift to be credible. "I — I'm just nervous. Jackson heard that we had a few beers together and started to question me."

"What did you tell him?" Frank inquired, even sterner now, his casual stance slowly looking as if he was blocking the room's only exit by intention.

"Nothing, really, I..." Benedict started but then trailed off. He took a long moment to carefully study Frank's face from below his long lashes before he asked, "You and von Biehn, are you... You are... close, aren't you? Very close."

This boy was dangerous, Frank suddenly realized. It took Frank a conscious effort to fight down the urge to walk across the room and break his neck. He had allowed himself to enjoy a friendly evening with a nice chap, had allowed himself to feel like a human being for a change and this was what he got in return. If their relationship came out, it would vaporize any chance of Frank helping Johann to come out of this alive.

"What did you tell him?!" Frank asked once more, not willing to confirm or deny the suspicion in any way.

Yet once again, he was surprised by Benedict's reaction. He blushed, and it definitely was a blush of embarrassment, not shame.

"I really have to go now," Benedict said softly, taking up the tray with the coffee and some cups, still crimson as a rose. "Please. He's already waiting."

But Frank didn't move. What the hell had happened? He was somehow sure that he and Johann wouldn't have anything to fear from Benedict, but as for the why, he was truly clueless.

"Frank, please!" Benedict insisted as Frank continued to block the door. "I really didn't tell him anything that would harm your case."

"But then what did you tell him?" Frank asked, this time a rather amused tone to his voice.

"I..." If possible, Benedict blushed even deeper. Softly, so only Frank would be able to hear it, the young man said, "I admitted to having a crush on you... He won't ask me anything about you ever again, I think."

For a second, Frank was plain speechless. Actually, he was so stunned that he didn't even object when Benedict sneaked his way past him through the door, balancing the tray and its contents with expert skill. Only in the very last moment, he reacted, catching the assistant by his sleeve.

"Why?" Frank asked, his voice still husky with surprise. "Why would you help us?"

"We shouldn't have to hide who we love, don't you think?" Benedict replied smoothly without really looking back. Gently, he pulled away from Frank's grip and then busily strode down the corridor.

It took Frank several moments to realize that Benny had said "we."

***

August 1943, Spreewald, von Biehn manor
Of course, Frank didn't stay in the bedroom as he had been told.

He had gone back there initially, but then sat on the corner of the bed, wondering if it had been a good idea to trust Johann, after all.

In the end, it was plain, old curiosity that won out against any better sense or knowledge.

So Frank slid out of the room again, listening for any conversation he could overhear, or any other noises that would warn him there was something wrong. At first, it felt as if the place was completely deserted, not a single sound to be heard in the early morning. But then there was von Biehn's voice, bellowing with rage, and Frank couldn't suppress the smile that involuntarily crept onto his face. Apparently, the unexpected visitor was currently getting a tremendous portion of Johann's not so friendly mood.

"You brainless idiot!" he heard him shout in German, somewhere in front of the manor. "Who the hell do you think you are?"

There was such honest-to-earth anger in Johann's voice that Frank had to admire his sheer guts. If anybody got a whiff of what really was going on, no connections whatsoever would be able to save Johann's neck. And yet, he was out there, delivering a performance with such gusto that it would have reaped stellar reviews on any stage.

"Who sent you here?" von Biehn demanded outside, repeating a little louder as apparently no satisfactory answer was delivered on the spot; "On whose orders are you here?!"

As stealthily as he could, Frank slipped down the hallway, hoping to catch a glimpse of the visitor. Johann made enough noise to give him a rather accurate idea of where they had to be standing.

Together with the huge windows and the rather opulent flower boxes they were sporting, it wasn't too hard to find a place where Frank was sure not to be spotted by accident.

Outside, in the brilliant morning sun, Frank could see Johann standing there in nothing but the shorts he had been wearing. Red with anger, he faced a young man in uniform who didn't look at all as if he had expected this kind of welcome.

"So if the letter requesting all participants to respect my wish of some solitude to prepare the meeting has been signed by the Reichsmarschall himself — you think this doesn't apply to you?"

Now the young man was actually blushing, though it looked as if he did so out of pure anger.

"You know perfectly well that I am the Reichsmarschall's aide de champs," the surprise visitor spat back with enough emphasis to make his neatly parted hair fall into his face, "and you know why I am here."

"I don't give a damn on why you are here, boy," Johann retorted coldly, making a great show of how utterly unimpressed he was, and managing pretty well. "Now get off my grounds!"

Once again, Frank had to force down a chuckle. If nothing else, German was a great language to yell and curse in. But as much fun as it was to watch Johann cut down the other guy's ego a size or two, the young man had identified himself as aide de champs of the Reichsmarschall. Being the Nazi equivalent of the Secretary of Defense, Göring was a tremendously busy person considering the kind of war the Germans were currently waging all over Europe. And usually meddling in an affair that until now would have been a mostly diplomatic thing definitely would have had no place in his schedule, unless of course the meeting which would be taking place here was far more than what Frank's employers had initially expected.

In the light of this new information, Johann's earlier comment that there would be someone much more important attending this meeting gained a completely different weight. It could be Göring himself attending the meeting, and that once again was a pretty interesting thing as far as Frank was concerned. If he would be able to take out the head of the German military, it would be a blow the Allied forces would profit from tremendously.

It took only moments until the bubbling sound of the boat's motor disrupted the relative silence again, followed by the muted sounds of a final shout-out at the pier.

Well, at least this was as he had been briefed on, Frank thought with another chuckle. Johann was high-up in the ranks, very assertive when it came to getting what he wanted and not shy of pointed arguments. In a way, Frank was sure that his commanding officers hadn't had old rapiers in mind when talking about pointed arguments, but it was a very apt image.

Slowly, he rose from his crouching position under the window, rather sure there wouldn't be any other surprise visitors on the grounds right then. Frank had well noted various weapons in the hall, mounted there between the old paintings and flags. All the blades were in good shape, and definitely no mere decoration, but he had never thought Johann would actually be using any of them. But assuming anything about von Biehn was proving a trickier business by the minute. That man Johann had just chased off the island probably had been wise not to continue tempting his fate.

Shaking his head, Frank had to admit to himself that he was growing fond of von Biehn, in all his dashing, confusing, making-no-sense-at-all ways. Which, in a way, was worse than falling in love, because it kept you thinking clearly and tended to last much longer.

Not good.

But not really bad, either.

On a windowsill next to the entrance, Frank spotted a bright blue pack of *Nil* cigarettes, together with a box of matches. Without much hesitation, he took out one of them and walked out onto the flight of stairs in front of the doorway.

So when Johann returned from the pier at a leisurely pace, he found his guest leaning against the door-frame,

Had Johann seriously thought that Frank would abandon his mission? Just because he asked nicely, was great in bed and said he was in love with him?

With a soundless sigh, Frank slumped to the ground and leaned his back against the wall below the window.

If he survived this madness, Frank silently swore to himself, he would quit this job. Maybe there would be a younger, more enthusiastic and less hormone-driven killer willing to take his place.

"I said, get off my grounds!" he heard Johann bellow again, this time with a serious threat in his voice. "I don't care what you want, I don't care who you are, and as long as it isn't Monday next week, I won't be seeing your face around here again!"

Apparently, the young man's answer once again wasn't what Johann had wanted to hear, for Frank could hear him roar in anger. Only a second later, the entrance door was slammed open by a frighteningly convincing berserker who had a vague similarity to the German Oberst Frank was currently living with. With long strides, von Biehn crossed the entrance hall and snatched an ancient rapier from one of the walls, very much giving the impression he knew how to handle it.

As swiftly as he had entered the place, Johann was out again, sword in hand, yelling, "Now get lost, you *nutzloser Schleimscheißer*, or I'll make you!"

This time, even Frank's rather extensive knowledge of German swearwords was sorely strained, but the way Johann hurled the expression at the other man was all the explanation one could need. Rapidly retreating footsteps on the gravel path signaled that the uniformed assistant had finally gotten the clue and made his way back to the boat he had arrived in. He didn't leave without his share of swearwords and threats, all of them countered by Johann in the same arrogant tone he had borne the whole time.

smoking, wearing nothing but the trousers he had worn the last evening and a lopsided smirk.

"*Nutzloser Schleimscheißer?*" Frank asked with deep amusement as Johann stopped a few meters away.

"Well, could you have thought of anything more fitting?" von Biehn shot back, shouldering his blade that Frank only now noticed was an officer's saber, not a rapier. "And shouldn't you be waiting in the bedroom?"

"I can see you liking that thought. But since when do I obey orders?" Frank asked sardonically. "Is he gone now?"

Johann nodded calmly. "For now, yes. He'll return and be much more of a nuisance than he already was, but not before next week."

There were so many questions burning in Frank to be asked he couldn't make up his mind on where to start. Why the Reichsmarschall? Why the bloody hell did Johann expect Frank not to continue his mission? What was going on here?

But in the bright light of the increasingly warm August morning, with the lawn glittering with dew and the faint scent of roses in the air, some things suddenly seemed more important to Frank. All else could wait until there was no other choice left. Maybe it wasn't such a good idea to spoil what little time they could have together.

"What about we take a swim before breakfast?" Frank suddenly suggested somewhat out of the blue, making Johann blink with surprise.

"Sure," von Biehn replied, insecure but happy about the sudden offer.

"Business" could be talked about any time later, Frank decided, and there were much nicer subjects one could imagine.

Johann's smile widened to a most charming grin as he took the saber off his shoulder and rammed it into the lawn. Turning his attention back to Frank, he walked over and took the cigarette out of the other man's fingers, taking a long drag himself.

"The water is cool and shallow here," Johann explained with a deep look into Frank's eyes. "But very refreshing."

"I'm sure we'll find a way to warm up again," Frank said suggestively, smirking at von Biehn.

***

September 1946, Nuremberg, Ms Haselönner's B&B
"Ach, Herr Hawthorne, Sie sind ja doch schon wach. Schönen guten Morgen!"

Apparently, Frau Haselönner, the charming, elderly lady who ran the tiny bed and breakfast Frank was staying in, had been waiting for him to come down for breakfast. Short and rather chubby, with curly white hair and an easy smile, she was making a little money out of her house by renting some of the spare rooms to foreigners. With her husband and both her sons dead in the war, and all these foreigners swarming the city, this was about the smartest thing she could do.

But right now, she was wiping her hands dry on her crisp white apron, gesturing him to wait a second.

"Da ist Post für Sie gekommen," she said ominously while fetching a rather battered-looking envelope from the sideboard, *"aus Amerika."*

A letter from America. *Now this was unexpected news indeed. Whoever had sent it knew where he was staying,* Frank thought, *and that left only a tiny circle of suspects.* Frau Haselönner handed him the envelope, and it took him only a split second to identify the sender.

The letter bore the seal of the U.S. Army, and he had already received more than one of their kind. And the fact that it was from his superiors in the army instead of the Office of the Secretary of Defense where he had sent his last appeal didn't bode well at all.

"*Ich hoffe, es sind gute Nachrichten...*" Frau Haselönner said softly, her eyes sympathetic and suddenly bare of all mirth. Hopefully, it's good news... She must have received her share of bad news in pretty similar letters, Frank realized.

"*Bestimmt,*" he replied, to his own surprise with a catching voice. Sure, he had said, while he was too worried to even open the letter here and now.

But his landlady only nodded with an understanding look. Silently, she turned around towards the kitchen, politely leaving him alone at the foot of the staircase. Some things were hard enough without strangers watching, and she was offering Frank what little comfort she could.

Frank sat down on the second to the last step, fingering the envelope. This letter would decide the outcome of Johann's trial, not the votes of the judges. For good or for bad, he was holding his lover's fate in his hands, and Frank wasn't sure if he wanted to make it real and final by opening the envelope.

He remained sitting on the stairs for a long time.

Chapter 9
Thunderstorm

August 1943, Spreewald, von Biehn Manor
Laughing tears, Frank let himself fall back into the high grass that surrounded them.

"You really did?" he asked incredulously when he had calmed down sufficiently. "I would have loved to see Göring's face that moment."

"I bet you would. It was priceless." Next to him, Johann was sitting on his heels, grinning with glee. "Hermann needed the whole weekend until he admitted I had been right."

Hermann... Inwardly, Frank shook his head, stunned. He seriously was sitting next to a man who was on first name terms with the Reichsmarschall! And yet, what a lovely day it had been so far...

They had taken a swim, and "warmed up again" on the lawn in front of the manor. They had breakfast in the kitchen, with Johann telling stories of his time at the university in Heidelberg, and both had shared their memories of their worst day at school. Frank had never known anyone he could so easily talk to as Johann.

Sometime around noon, Johann had suggested they take a walk, and much to Frank's amazement had managed to arrange a surprise picnic for the two of them. Somewhere on a sunlit clearing among the ancient trees, they had "coincidentally" come across a blanket and a basket with bread and cheese and wine; von Biehn utterly unconvincing in his attempts to appear uninvolved.

Since then, they had been sitting here, watching the dragonflies buzz across the water of a nearby stream, and chatting about close to everything. Of course, politics and "business" had been no subject at all, even though it had been tremendously hard at times, given their respective lifestyles. But so far, they had managed with sufficient grace.

Frank had told him some of his adventures in northern Africa, while Johann had recalled some anecdotes of his time as a student in Heidelberg. Like the one time he and his friend Armin had scandalized their fraternity by showing up to a rather official event with a *transvestite* and a black exotic dancer as their respective plus ones. And despite the occasional awkward silences, it had been an afternoon full of laughter and pleasant companionship. It felt weird to Frank to realize that even though they passionately disagreed on some subjects, they had a lot in common. Especially when it came to things that were important to them, they were of one heart. Heavens, they even agreed on which things were to be considered important!

Thoughtful, Frank blinked up into the sky as, suddenly, the sun disappeared behind a cloud. Frowning, he studied the heavy, roiling clouds that had so far managed to completely evade their attention.

"Johann," he asked, "is it normal that the clouds here have that sickly, yellow tinge?"

Craning his neck, Johann looked up at the sky as well, cursing under his breath.

"*Ach Scheiße.*"

There honestly was a faint, sulfur colored tinge to the dark gray underside of the cloud, and apparently, it wasn't a good thing.

"What's wrong?" Frank asked as Johann started to pack the remains of their extended meal.

"Heavy thunderstorm, maybe hail." Von Biehn replied briefly, looking up at the clouds once again. "Probably hail."

Then suddenly, an unexpectedly sharp gust of cool air rushed through the trees, making the old oaks groan. In the distance, the soft rolling of thunder could be heard and within no more than a minute, the warm August afternoon had become distinctively fresh.

"What is this kind of weather?" Frank asked while helping Johann to gather their stuff in haste.

"Average German August weather for you, I'd say." Packing up both the blanket and basket, he pointed towards a narrow path leading back to the manor's island. "You'll get the loveliest weather on earth here in August, but then suddenly, it flips over, and this is what you get. It'll be over in less than an hour, but until then, we better seek shelter."

Within moments, the sunlight faded even more, blotted out by roiling clouds dark and oddly colorful. The next crash of thunder was much louder than the one before, rolling over them like a tangible force. Together with the wine and the good company, this unexpected display of nature's force made Frank feel giddy, electrified with the sight and the smells and the sounds of it all.

But as a good guest, he grabbed his walking-cane and stood up, no longer bothering to pretend he still had problems walking on his own. It would only look silly considering that he apparently was feeling almost perfectly fine when they had sex. And Frank could have hardly cared less right now.

They had barely managed a few meters when the first heavy drops of rain started to fall, a few at first, then hundreds, then too many to count. Without a word, Johann grabbed Frank by the arm and dragged him below the canopy of a massive copper beech tree. The thick roof of chocolate-colored leaves offered at least some protection against the heavy rain, and for a few moments, both of them stood there next to the gnarled trunk, staring at the masses of water pouring down.

"Wow..." Frank commented wryly, shaking the water out of his hair. "Not bad."

"Not really the kind of finale I had in mind for the picnic," Johann added, "but not bad, indeed."

With a deafening bang, lightning struck somewhere close by, light and sound arriving almost simultaneously. If possible at all, the rain fell even harder, turning the path into a small creek.

"So what were you planning as a finale?"

Von Biehn grinned, that kind of sleazy, delicious grin Frank had already learned to identify as a rather indecent invitation. For a moment, it looked as if Johann was still pondering the best answer, but then Johann put down the basket. Grabbing Frank by his shirt, von Biehn pulled him into a close embrace, kissing him passionately, full of hunger and none too gentle.

With the wine, the thunderstorm and the rest of events, this kiss was nothing less than scorching. This was indeed the way both of them had wanted the afternoon to end, and the downpour didn't make one bit of a difference. Within less than a moment, Frank found himself clawing at Johann's shirt, fumbling with the buttons as the moist cotton definitely wasn't intent on letting go. And Johann laughed into their kiss, his hands all over Frank's back, strong and full of desire.

Finally, Frank gave up on subtlety, ripping the annoying piece of cloth where the buttons didn't yield to his craving fingers. Once again, von Biehn laughed, obviously pleased by the turn of events. Johann, of course, didn't even try to bother with opening Frank's shirt the proper way, instead pulling it over his lover's head in a single motion that spoke of way too much experience for a decent man.

Not that Frank minded.

But the shirt, of course, got stuck as Frank was about to pull it over his wrists, as Johann hadn't thought of the buttons at the cuffs. Yet a swift look in Johann's sparkling green eyes told Frank that it hadn't been a coincidence. With almost gleeful malice, von Biehn continued to pull the shirt down Frank's back, effectively creating makeshift handcuffs.

For a moment, they stood there, chest against chest, breathing hard, their eyes locked. Around them, the world was disappearing behind a gray curtain of heavy rain, and slowly, it was coming through underneath the tree as well. Neither of them moved as the first heavy, lukewarm drops hit them, a welcome caress on their burning skin.

Frank had the smell of Johann in his nose, all sunlight and grass, wine and sweat and sweet desire. He loved the way he could feel the other man's heart beat against his own chest, how his arms held him immobile in the increasingly heavy rain. Soon, a small trickle of water ran down his back between his shoulder blades, following his spine and dissolving into a cool spot once it reached the waistband of his trousers. The water was refreshing, invigorating, cleansing, and together with the roaring noise of the rain on the canopy of leaves above them, it was very easy to forget all those things that didn't matter right here and now.

"Close your eyes," von Biehn said softly, as close to a whisper as he could in the noise.

There were only very few things Frank would have preferred, so he did as he was told, eager to find out what Johann had in mind. For another moment, nothing happened, except maybe for von Biehn pressing his increasingly hard dick against Frank's hip. But then Johann leaned forward, nibbling at the soft skin underneath Frank's ear, covering him with gentle bites all the way down to his shoulder. Each touch felt like an electric jolt, so very desired and yet so surprisingly intense when it finally happened.

Only when Johann didn't restrain himself any longer and bit down hard enough to pierce the other man's skin, Frank reacted with a hiss. Not willing to stand still any longer, Frank pulled out of the restraining embrace, stripping off his shirt with no care whether it survived the procedure or not. His lover still only smirked, his hands wandering along Frank's chest as if they still had to decide where to really start business.

But Frank didn't have any such doubts.

With a deft motion, he grabbed Johann, turning him around until he leaned back against the trunk of the tree. Both were breathing hard, their eyes reflecting each others' wordless, burning desire. Planting his hands on both sides of Johann's head, Frank kissed him once again with all the passion he felt, wild and unrestrained as the weather around them. He didn't care about the fact that by now, it was raining almost as hard underneath the beech as it was outside. All Frank cared for was Johann, and the overwhelming urge to get rid of their remaining clothes.

Growling with lust, Frank pressed Johann against the damp bark, reveling in the sensation of the other man's chest pressed against his own, of his cock pressing hot and hard against the stiff flesh he could feel in Johann's trousers. It was only a matter of seconds until he was unfastening the belt and opening the buttons that were the last barrier to his pleasure. With Johann's eager help, they got the completely soaked fabric open, not bothering with shoes or anything else. Frank noticed how his lover repeatedly tried to get into his pants respectively, but each time lost his mental cohesion when Frank managed to stroke Johann's throbbing dick in just the right way, and it made him grin with malicious glee. It was bliss to see a man as resourceful and assertive as von Biehn reduced to a puddle of shivering desire in his hands, deeply satisfying bliss.

Just as another wave of thunder rolled over them, pounding their chests with the pure impact of sound, he grabbed Johann again and spun him around to face the tree. It proved a little more difficult than expected, as Johann's trousers were now a wet bundle wrapped rather unfortunately around his ankles, but neither of them cared for grace right now. Seeing Johann leaning forward, his hands against the giant trunk of the beech, his ass invitingly tilted in just the right way made Frank growl with enthusiasm. This was beyond passionate; it was feral, primal, but so...perfect. It was what they both wanted, what they needed, and no words were necessary.

Raking his fingernails across Johann's back, Frank pressed his still-wrapped dick against the other man's ass, a wide dirty grin plastered all over his face. Johann growled in response, though it sounded mostly like an order not to let him wait any longer. Reflexively, Frank decided that he wouldn't rush things and instead of finally unbuttoning his own pants, he started to caress his lover's balls, his crack, his ass. He reached around Johann and grabbed his throbbing dick, massaging the hot flesh until the other man groaned and shivered with need.

Smirking, Frank let his free hand trail down Johann's crack, teasing his entrance with two fingers. Wet as they were, it was easy to push them inside, and Johann's responsive growl felt rather rewarding. Not wasting too much time on preparations, Frank barely ensured that he would be able to enter his lover without doing too much damage. Then he unbuttoned his pants, finally freeing his cock from its confines, rubbing it to full hardness.

Without a word, he pushed his dick inside his lover, as swiftly and deeply as the matters allowed, now groaning himself with satisfaction. Johann rested with his head against the trunk of the tree, his fingers looking as if clawing into the bark, simultaneously moaning and cursing and cheering under his breath.

Again, Frank thrust into his lover, deeper this time, harder, almost painful but too engulfed in passion to care. He wanted to do him thoroughly; wanted to get lost in his desire and completely forget everything else. And Johann made it so easy...

By now, it was raining underneath the tree just as hard as outside, the only difference being the fact that underneath the beech, the heavy drops and first grains of hail additionally carried the occasional little twig or leaf. It was silly, and far from comfortable or romantic, and yet Frank wouldn't have wanted it any other way.

Thrusting in hard, he increased his momentum, feeling his dick glide in and out of Johann; feeling himself move inside the other man; reveling in the sensation. He held von Biehn firmly by his waist, not allowing him the freedom to move one inch. He took control of Johann in the most fundamental way possible, and Frank loved every single second of it, every hard shove.

Already, he had to watch out not to come instantly, but that wasn't the way he wanted this to end. Instead, Frank pulled Johann up again, holding him around his chest, Frank's cock still deeply buried inside the other man. Von Biehn was panting and glowing with heat despite the rain and the hail, his ragged breath sounding like a caress; as if calling out Frank's name without using the word. It was obvious that Johann didn't need much more to come either, already rubbing his own cock with grim need. But Frank reached around and took those hands away, continuing to bring his lover to completion. He wanted to feel it as close as possible, to be there with every sense available.

Giving a loud groan, von Biehn let his head fall back onto Frank's shoulder, his pelvis working in union with his lover's hands. Frank could feel Johann approach his climax with giant strides, both with his hands and his own dick. He could feel how Johann grew tighter and tighter around him, and he didn't need Johann's bellowing roar to let him know how his lover felt. Finally, with jerking thrusts, von Biehn reached his release, his hands clawing against Frank's sides, his body so taut its tension seemed to seep over into Frank. Feeling the other man's semen slick in his own hands, Frank didn't hold back any longer, releasing the tension that had built up inside of him in what had felt like ages, bliss washing over him like the pouring rain as he came inside his lover.

***

September 1946, Nuremberg, Ms Haselönner's B&B

All morning, Frank had been angry. Furious, to say the least.

He couldn't recall the last time he had been that enraged. Never before on his missions, however dreadful or hopeless the situation might have looked, had he been this angry. But the letter this morning had been simply too much.

As already feared, the letter's contents had been negative, and after a long, long time of sitting on Frau Haselönner's stairs, Frank had come to the conclusion that he had run out of options. The letter had contained nothing but a formal rejection of his request and a stiff reminder to stick to the chain of command next time he produced any other document. It could have been worded far less politely, but the news was devastating nonetheless.

The whole idea of him coming here had been to stand witness in the trial for Johann, and as soon as he had made his intention known to his superiors, things had become ugly. Suddenly, Frank had been explicitly ordered not to say a single word about what happened during his time in Johann's manor or why he had apparently aborted his mission. That they practically condemned an honorable man to death hadn't mattered one bit.

Frank had gone quite some miles to get things moving again, but apparently there had been graver reasons than the life of a man. Political reasons. Wherever he had pleaded his cause, the only answer had been: "This is a highly classified mission you are talking about, Captain, and you are not to disclose any of it in a public trial."

It had taken Frank a long, long time to accept that apparently sending an innocent man to his death was easier on the conscience of some people than admitting they had accepted help from him in winning this war. A German man, of all people.

It sounded so unbelievable at first. But the more Frank ended up with nothing but sympathetic smiles, the more he got used to the thought that politics sometimes were more important than morals.

In the end, he had left for Nuremberg with nothing but his hopes to help Johann. Right before leaving, he had posted a rather desperate letter to the Ministry of Defense, hoping that he would at least stir up some dust. But since this morning, even that little hope had been crushed.

Which didn't leave Frank with many options if he wasn't going to sit silent while watching Johann as he was executed. He might have been quite effectively barred from being any help for Johann in the trials, but that didn't mean he was completely without resources.

He just was out of ideas.

In the end, Frank decided that he had to come up with other approaches that might offer new hope. His first pick had been Elias, but the lawyer had only been as calm and sympathetic and non-committal as ever. Nothing Frank, with his boiling temper, could relate to right then.

He had to do something; something productive, anything that made being here worthwhile for Johann and himself. And yet, all his professional experience had been concerned with getting rid of people, not saving them.

Frank did have an idea. Not really a useful plan, but maybe the beginning of one. It was fact that if he didn't give evidence that Johann had been working against the Hitler regime the whole time, the judges would have no choice but to fully agree with the sentence demanded by the prosecution.

Consequentially, that left either the judges' choice or the prosecution's demand to meddle with if the original combination didn't suit his taste.

Even if Frank could manage to sway the judges' opinions, it would look more than questionable if they decided different to what Jackson had pleaded. And looking decent, civilized and just was what this whole trial was all about. So somehow, he had to involve Jackson in his plot, knowingly or not.

And the way to a man always led through the one who made his coffee...

Chapter 10
Desperate Measures

August 1943, Spreewald, von Biehn's manor
The thunderstorm had passed as swiftly as it had come up, but it had left the park surrounding Johann's manor thoroughly disheveled. Everywhere, small branches had broken off the trees, and in some places, hail had piled up in what looked like little snowdrifts. In the cool air, mist rose rapidly from the still heated ground, with long trailing whiffs reaching up like tentacles of a ghostly, giant octopus. It was an eerie moment, to say the least.

Frank and Johann had finally separated again in relative silence, but not without kisses that spoke of more affection than just physical gratification. They had gathered up their clothes, and took off what they had left on in the heat of the moment. As there was no one else on the island anyway, they continued their way back to the manor completely naked, grimacing at the occasional ice under their feet.

For a long time, they walked together in silence, each one lost in their thoughts and the mellow feeling of sexual satiation. Trying not to be too obvious, Frank watched Johann, intrigued by the fact that slowly, he was beginning to wonder if after the war, they might see each other again. Not in terms of "by chance," but actively going back to Germany and trying to seek him out.

Frank couldn't tell if he would, right then, but it was a nice prospect, and yet the feeling somehow scared him. All his life, he had been a solitary person, not really attached to anyone or anything, and that was what had made it possible for him to do what he did in the very first place. Marrying some poor woman to distract from his "affliction" had never been an option to him. And now suddenly having someone he possibly wanted to share the rest of his life with was...

It implied more changes than Frank would have liked.

But then again, the war was far from being over, and chances that either of them would survive were marginal at best. Very marginal.

Frank must have sighed softly at the thought, for Johann suddenly looked up at him, a melancholic and understanding smile on his lips.

"It's hard to ignore it," Johann said gently, turning his eyes back to their path. "As much as we try, reality comes creeping back into our world again and again."

Frank nodded, not really knowing what to add to the thought. Reality was the only problem in their relationship so far, but my, what a problem that was.

"We have to talk." Von Biehn's remark came unexpected, and the way he put it made it clear it was about business this time.

Frank nodded, unable to suppress a smirk at their current situation, asking, "Now? Here? Naked?"

Johann chuckled softly. "I think we are both heading for a decent shower, but on the way there, we might as well talk."

For another moment, they continued their walk, now finally reaching areas of the park that were already familiar to Frank.

"I'm listening," Frank stated, as von Biehn made no attempts to explain any of the many questions they had so industriously ignored over the last days. Johann smiled once again, nodding.

"Do you know why all these high-up people are going to come here?"

"To receive new orders, I assume," Frank replied, adding on a wry note, "If we had any intelligence on this, it wasn't considered necessary to the fulfillment of my task."

"Little surprise at that." Biting his lower lip, von Biehn was apparently trying to think of how to sum up a lot of things in a few words. "Over the last few years, I have been working on a study commissioned by the Reichsmarschall personally, on a strictly need-to-know basis. Which meant him, Adolf, and my humble self."

Raising a surprised eyebrow, Frank wondered once again if his people back at home had at least a vague idea on how wrong they were concerning the person of Oberst von Biehn.

"It was a study about transportation efficiency, and it is finished by now."

"That sounds positively boring," Frank remarked flat out, triggering a beaming smile in von Biehn's face.

"That's the point," Johann replied, apparently endlessly pleased by Frank's comment. "But take into consideration that transportation always means troop transportation as well, and that the area covered by the study reaches from Porto to Moscow and from Hammerfest to Dakar."

The sheer size of the project made Frank blink with irritation. At first, he had thought Johann was talking about one of those German pet projects on how to make things work efficiently in general, but now it sounded... different. Huge. And considering that von Biehn was involved, probably very dangerous.

"A map?" he asked as the pieces of information connected in his head.

"Precisely. Although most of the study is nothing but a gargantuan heap of numbers, the result basically is a map of Europe and northern Africa." Delicately picking a dark leaf from Frank's naked behind, Johann continued, "As long as there is no enemy contact, I can tell you exactly how long it'll take for any kind and number of troops to get from A to B anywhere on this map. Plus or minus half an hour."

The implications of Johann's boastful claim made Frank gape. If it was really possible to gather and process such an incredible amount of reliable intelligence, German troops in the future would be able to move across the continent in a speed unmatched by any other army. They would turn into the proverbial hedgehog, already there wherever the poor rabbit finally arrived. The thought was plain scary.

"Of course," von Biehn added, "this only is an advantage as long as the Allies have no access to that information."

"And that is where I come into play," Frank stated, still stunned but relieved beyond words that finally, things were beginning to make sense.

"Absolutely." With astonishing affection, Johann nudged Frank's shoulder, smiling at him. "Can you imagine how I felt, standing on my balcony, praying for a way to get this information into the "right" hands? And then suddenly, there was an angel falling from the skies, bringing with him the chance I had asked for, taking my heart in return?"

"I..." Frank started, once again feeling overrun by von

Biehn's rather poetic description of events. "No. But I think I get your point."

Von Biehn's smile was bittersweet and he nodded. "Charming as ever, and honest to the bone."

Once again, a few moments passed without either of them saying a word. If Johann was honest about his studies, and by now Frank had no doubt about that, continuing on his mission as planned would be foolish. The meeting would be considered compromised, and the data of the study as well. And it would make it much harder for Frank to return safely, which suddenly had become more important than ever before.

The only thing that irked Frank was that von Biehn apparently had it all thought out from the very beginning, and everything turned out the way he wanted it; even the odd assassin falling in love with him. Giving him an awkward sidelong glance, Frank wondered how much Johann had actually planned, how much of his actions were just what they seemed to be and how much were merely there to make him act the way Johann wanted. Was Johann also wondering if there would be a life after the war for them?

"Why do you do this?" Frank suddenly asked.

"Do what?"

"Commit treason against your country."

Johann gave a bitter snort, shaking his head.

"I don't," he replied firmly, pausing his walk to gesture at the manor that rose ahead of them from the mist across the park. "This has been the home of my family for generations. The whole area belonged to us for centuries, and we have taken care of it ever since. This is my country, and I don't commit treason against it when I help in getting the place rid of the worst plague I have ever seen."

There was such a barely contained, passionate anger in von Biehn's voice that Frank was genuinely surprised. He had already known that Johann didn't harbor any special sympathies with the Nazi regime, but that he despised them to such a degree was new.

"Whenever doubts become a crime," Johann continued, "whenever parents become afraid their children might turn them in; a country where the power of the government is mired inextricably with the jurisdiction and the executive, where you have three secret polices spying on the population and people disappear without a word, that is not my country." Looking firmly at Frank, Johann concluded, "My country and Nazi Germany, those are two very different places. And I dearly hope I'll live to see the day when the latter one falls."

***

September 1946, Nuremberg, on the roof opposing Jackson's quarters

It was as late at night as it would become, and yet still there was light in the rooms Chief Prosecutor Jackson occupied for the duration of the trials. Didn't that man ever go to bed?

Crouching low on the roof of an old building opposite the hotel Jackson was accommodated in, Frank once again wondered if he was taking it too far now. His talks with Benedict that afternoon originally had been as dispiriting as the rest of the day. Jackson seemed to be a strictly business person, married to his profession and without an ounce of an exploitable fault.

Frank was rather sure that he would be able to persuade Benny to help them save Johann's life if he only asked, but he didn't want to involve the boy as long as it wasn't the last option.

But in the end, there was something Benedict had said that rang a bell inside Frank's mind. Jackson might be a harsh man, and had often enough made a point of stating that he didn't necessarily believe in granting a foreigner, especially a former enemy of war, the same judicial rights as every American citizen. But to the core of his being, he seemed to believe in justice, in doing the right thing.

It took Frank quite a while to accept that Benny might be right on that one. In Frank's mind, the Chief Prosecutor had been merely on a witch-hunt, trying to bring down Frank's lover at any cost. But even Frank had to admit that this maybe had been a slightly biased view.

Maybe Jackson really was trying to do what he believed was right, and it was simply the lack of proper information that made him act like he did.

Well, he would find out tonight.

***

August 1943, Spreewald, von Biehn manor
"Come on, turn around, and let me scrub your back."

Johann's friendly order came unexpected, but definitely not unwelcome to Frank. They had returned to the manor and checked for any damages the thunderstorm might have left. But nothing worse had happened than some puddles underneath an open window, so the two men had retired to more pleasant tasks.

Like getting their well-deserved hot shower.

Naturally, that meant sharing a shower, and so Frank peacefully turned around, leaning his arms against the tiled wall and let Johann scrub his back. The air was filled with moisture and the heady scent of the lemon soap Johann was using; the water pouring from the shower a constant, relaxing murmur.

Once again, Frank realized that he was thinking fondly of sharing the rest of his life with the other man, and it was an unsettling thought. He had never felt this at ease with any of his partners, never as naturally trusting and calm. Having Johann around was like feeling complete, content for the first time in his life.

But of course, it would never be.

Probably, one of them would be killed before the war was over, possibly both of them. And even if — however this would end — after the war they would end up on different sides, one a victor, the other one defeated. Nothing Frank wanted to think of right then, all he wanted to feel was the firm hand of Johann, cleaning and caressing him in equal parts, tracing the various scars on his body and yet not inquiring about them.

"You know what bothers me?" Johann suddenly asked, not as seriously as Frank's gloomy thoughts would have demanded. "There is... the study I have been speaking of earlier, yes?"

Johann sounded as if he wasn't sure on how to say what he had on his mind, and that alone was a rare thing. Frank turned around and looked at his lover, but all he could see in the other man's eyes was a sparkling mischief so deep it was sexy.

"It's wrong."

"What is wrong?"

"The study. There's a mistake."

For a long moment, Johann's remark didn't make any sense to Frank, especially since he seemed not too worried about it.

"You see," Johann continued to explain, still gesturing with the sponge in his hand, "it's nothing big. Just two accidentally flipped numbers, a simple mistake."

"A complete coincidence," Frank guessed, and got a lively nod from Johann in return.

"Absolutely. And I am completely oblivious of its existence."

"Of course."

Johann nodded, apparently waiting for any other reaction from Frank other than a vaguely confused stare. Frank's expression didn't change, though, so Johann continued, "The two flipped numbers are in a figure used to denote the strength of concrete. And the faulty paper was one of those that the bridge quality calculations in France were based on." Smiling, Johann added, "It is just a tiny difference, but enough to make smaller bridges judged two categories better than they actually would have deserved."

In Frank's head, the thoughts were racing. Once again, Johann in his perfectly cryptic way was trying to tell him something important, and he didn't really get it. It didn't help that they were both naked, under the shower, still dazed with the intensity of the sex they had just had.

Apparently, Johann had sneaked a deliberate mistake into his work, and was trying to tell him about it. Some misjudged bridges in France didn't sound like a big deal to Frank, though. But as it was Johann von Biehn he was talking to here, he was sure it was immense. He just didn't understand why.

"And that's a good thing?" he asked carefully, making Johann grin widely.

"That's a disaster." Wriggling his eyebrows, Johann asked, "What do you know about the roads in France?"

"Nothing really," Frank replied with a shrug, "except maybe that all major roads run like a star from Paris."

This time, Johann only looked at the wet man who shared his shower, his face clearly showing he expected Frank to get the idea himself.

"So according to your map," Frank said, voicing his thoughts, "you can move troops properly from Paris to anywhere else. But to go from anywhere else to a third place in France which isn't Paris, you'd need much longer than expected..."

"Absolutely."

Still Frank didn't really see the big thing about this, and finally Johann seemed to give up on his games.

"Adolf will have to fortify the French coastline against an invasion from England, at least as long as the isles aren't conquered. If they dare, that would be the place for the Allies to try and get an anchorhead. So there will be a lot of German troops lined up like pearls on a necklace."

Johann's hands painted the image of a coastline dotted with fortifications in the air, the pale foam on his hands in odd contrast to his tanned skin. But slowly, Frank realized where this was leading, and he gaped in amazement at the size of von Biehn's ambitions. Seeing the change on Frank's face, Johann grinned even wider, continuing, "So if I knew where the Germans misjudged the way they can move troops along the coast, I knew where I could strike as long as I could muster sufficient numbers. It would be bloody murder, but the German reinforcements could never arrive in time."

"Oh my God..." Frank whispered, still trying to come to terms with the scope of those ideas.

"There are some beaches in Normandy that should be possible to secure neatly even with an army as badly organized and inefficient as yours."

Right then, Frank felt like the proverbial rabbit himself. Wherever his line of thoughts led him, Johann had already been there and left a pointer in the next direction. If it was true what he had just said, and there was very little doubt von Biehn knew what he was talking of, he had just given the Allies the single most important piece of intelligence in the whole war; if he managed to get this information into the right hands. Which made surviving even more important.

"You are... dangerous." Frank remarked in plain awe. "Goddamn dangerous."

Now Johann only smiled sadly.

"I am lonely in my brilliance," he replied, only to get slapped by Frank with the sponge, suds flying everywhere in the bathroom.

"You are impossible. And so modest."

"Will you kiss me?" Johann replied, sneaking his arms around Frank's waist, warm and wet and strong and oh so welcome.

"Always."

***

September 1946, Nuremberg, Palace of Justice, prison wing
"Oh God, Johann, I don't know what else to do..."

Elias' soft words hung in Johann's prison cell like a condemnation. The slender lawyer was wringing his hands in nervous helplessness and looked as if he'd rather scream and run in circles.

Johann and Frank, both seemingly composed, were sitting on the chairs the guard had kindly provided, watching Elias as his nerves finally seemed to unravel; not that Frank hadn't seen that moment coming a long time already. Legally, there wasn't any possible twist or turn anyone could find to make Johann appear uninvolved with the whole war. Too often his name had signed the crucial plans and concepts. Sure, over the years, Johann had helped a lot of people to get out of Nazi Germany, probably saving all their lives, Frank and Elias among them. But would that be enough? In this kind of trial?

Most probably not. Rather, Jackson would call it a well-prepared insurance in case things went wrong the way they had. And would move on to his apparently endless list of crimes against humanity he thought von Biehn guilty of. At least that was what Jackson was supposed to do.

So it was little wonder that now, two days before the scheduled end of the hearings, Elias was as nervous as a man could possibly be. He was running out of options, and worse, out of ideas.

"I-" Elias choked, "I am so sorry."

Johann, so far, hadn't reacted to Elias' silent breakdown, but now nodded calmly. "It's alright, Elias. I knew what risk I was taking all the time. There is no fault of yours."

On his chair, Frank was close to grinding his teeth. On the one hand, he was burning to give Elias and Johann at least a hint of his conversation with Jackson last night. On the other hand, he had left there without anything substantial — so what was the point in telling? In the end, Frank decided to wait for a less public situation to inform the two. Even though the GI on guard wasn't outright leaning in the door frame this time, he was listening to every word they said out in the hallway.

"You know," Frank stated into the cell's leaden silence, "I always thought it was a German proverb that on sea and at court, you're in the hands of God."

Simultaneously, Johann and Elias turned around to face him, the slightly confused look on their faces almost comically identical.

"You should have a little more faith in the proceedings," Frank continued, knowing how weird he must sound to the other men. Especially as this normally had been Elias' line. "You haven't done anything unjust, so what should you be punished for?"

For a moment, his companions just continued staring at him in incredulous silence. Then, Elias mumbled, "That is not the way this works, dear."

"I never thought you were a religious kind of man," Johann remarked, more a question than a statement. Thoughts were racing behind his eyes; a reminder of that brilliant mind that had dazzled Frank three years ago.

He still loved him, Frank realized, he still loved him so much. Maybe false hope was better than no hope at all.

"Well, if you don't have faith in the judicial system, then..." Frank said with a hint of a knowing smirk, "why don't you have faith in me?"

It was a lie, Frank was very well aware of that. But seeing Johann's face light up with a smile that was at the same time proud and grateful, he knew he had done the right thing.

If they kill him, Frank thought to himself, *I have no idea how I'm going to survive.*

If the trial found Johann guilty, he would be hanged within a few days. Frank knew he couldn't let that happen. He couldn't allow anyone to harm the love of his life, even if that meant going against his own people, betraying the very country he had risked his life for so many times.

Breaking into the prison here at Nuremberg was ridiculously close to impossible, getting Johann and himself out again alive even more so. But Frank knew he would have to try if the judges found Johann guilty. He would die trying, most probably, but he wouldn't sit around idly waiting for his own people to kill the man he loved.

Frank sorely hoped there would be another way out of this mess.

Chapter 11
The Lovers

August 1943, Spreewald, von Biehn manor

Once again, a bright morning dawned over their little enchanted island. Fog was covering almost everything on the ground, and the crowns of the trees stood out like so many little green hills. Birds were chirping everywhere, and from somewhere to the south, the light breeze carried the scent of fresh fish being smoked.

Just like the days before, Frank had woken up well before Johann, who still slept like a child in his bed. *A rather well-used bed of late,* Frank thought with a smirk. Somewhere in the back of his mind, he had expected that the playful passion between him and Johann would burn out after a few days, but it was still there, unchanged if a little more refined. And living together was frighteningly easy. So many things went without saying. So many times they just seemed to read each other's mind.

And it didn't feel to Frank as if either of them was going out of his way to please the other one.

If they had met in different circumstances, he would be sure he just had met a man he'd happily live with for the rest of his life. There was so little doubt about this fact in Frank that it was unsettling. He had always assumed that his special "affliction" meant there would never be a special someone in his life, a better half. A husband, so to speak. But even though his mind still struggled with the fact, his heart already knew that Johann could be the one. Frank could see them grow old together, and it was an absurd and frightening and wonderful thing.

But that had not been what had kept him from snuggling against Johann's chest once more and trying to sleep for another hour.

Walking out onto the balcony of Johann's study, Frank grimaced at the dew under his naked feet. He really should have brought at least a shirt, he thought, wearing only the trousers of one of Johann's pajamas. It was amazing how cool it became here over night, especially compared with how hot it turned over the day.

Down in the park, Frank could already see the dark shape of "his" garden shed forming in the thinning mist, and thinking of the days he had spent there brought him back to his problem.

He had been sent here on a mission. A mission for his country, planned and decided upon by men much smarter than himself. Hopefully. And now there was Johann, who offered him a chance to stab a dagger right into the side of the whole German Reich, in exchange for abandoning what he was supposed to do here.

Make a silent exit, ensure that the information arrived safely back home. It was the much more sensible thing to do, if not exactly the simpler thing.

But was it the right thing as well?

Frank had given up figuring out Johann a long time ago when it came to his plans. And that was the problem. What if Johann had set up all this only to divert him from his mission? What if this was a simple ruse, blown up in proportion so Johann could get a good fuck out of it on the side? What if Johann was just using him like a pawn?

And falling in love with Johann definitely hadn't made things simpler, not one bit. It was very hard to stay rational when every inch of your mind longed so desperately for a happy ending.

"*Hey, Süßer...*" Johann's voice from the door came unexpected, but even now entirely welcome. Frank just loved having the other man around. "What are you doing out here?"

"Thinking," Frank replied without turning around.

Johann only mumbled something vaguely consenting and walked out onto the balcony as well. Gently, he slid his arms around Frank's waist from behind, hugging him tightly.

"Will you be thinking here some more time?" he asked, drawing Frank into a cuddly embrace. Johann wasn't wearing a shirt either, and his chest felt still warm as if he had come here directly out of bed. "Or should I start making breakfast?"

With a soundless sigh, Frank leaned against the other man.

If Johann really was doing all this just to make him believe his story, he was doing so with amazing commitment. And wasn't the chance that it might be for real much more important than that it might be a scam? Frank had killed more than enough people in his job, and until now there hadn't been a visible effect on the war or anything. Wouldn't it be wiser, then, to try a different approach for a change?

"I'll be with you in a minute, my love." Frank turned his head, planting a soft kiss on von Biehn's shoulder. "Just go ahead, make breakfast."

So, it was decided, Frank realized. He would abandon the set goal of his mission for nothing but the word of a German Nazi officer. And for the love of his life.

For a long while, the two men just stood there on the balcony, looking at the sun slowly eating away at the mists below them. The flowers in the planters on the balcony were still glittering with dew, but each time the air moved, it brought another promise of a hot August day to come.

"Didn't you want to go and make breakfast?" Frank finally asked.

"I will," Johann replied. But instead of leaving, Johann buried his nose against Frank's neck, covering his spine with tiny kisses, scratching and lovely, unshaven as he was.

Calmly, Frank closed his eyes, reveling in the sensation. The cool air on his skin, Johann's warmth around him; each touch a tiny gift. Johann's kisses wandered down from Frank's neck to his left shoulder, bit by bit in tiny, nibbling steps that seemed to send tingling waves across Frank's skin.

"You are aware that we're not going to get any breakfast this way?" Frank asked, though he couldn't have cared less about food right now. Instead, he brought his arms behind him and around Johann, caressing him gently. "Not that I am complaining."

"Thought so," Johann replied against Frank's shoulder, his voice a little mumbled and his stubble again delightfully scratching against the other man's skin. "There's a different kind of hunger I'd like to take care of first."

Smiling against Frank's skin, Johann pressed his hips against the other man's ass, the thin fabric of their pajamas hardly able to conceal anything, especially not Johann's hot and throbbing erection. Slowly, he let his hands wander down Frank's chest, letting them take their time to caress his nipples and to play with the hair on his stomach before they dived into Frank's pants.

Already half hard, it didn't take Johann long to get him to moan softly with desire, holding his cock firmly with one hand, Frank's chest with another, making sure there was as much skin contact between them as possible. They had learned a lot about each other during the last days, mostly how to pleasure each other in their favorite ways, and the experience showed in every single one of Johann's motions.

Frank, on the other hand, just savored the sensation, his head leaning back onto his lover's shoulder, his hands gently stroking along Johann's sides. For half a moment, he was worried to remain here outside on the balcony, but then — who should see them? There was no one else on the entire island, and they would hear any visitor long before anyone could possibly see them. And he hadn't wasted a single thought on this the other day during the thunderstorm. Still, it was an odd sensation standing so exposed, naughty and exciting at the same time.

When Johann pulled down his pants so that the thin cotton fabric pooled around his ankles, Frank had to laugh softly. The morning air felt cool around his exposed cock, but it also felt good. Still Johann was pressing his hard dick against Frank's ass, and once again, he wondered if maybe he was missing out on something there. So far, he hadn't allowed Johann to fuck him. Not that Johann had asked to be on top, or that he had seemed anything but happy to be on the receiving end of Frank's attentions.

But it was occasions like this one when Frank wondered if it wasn't time to drop his old habit of always remaining on top of things, in more ways than one. Until now, he had never felt safe enough with another man to feel really comfortable with taking the passive part in lovemaking. The few times he had been taken by other men had been... Suffice to say, he didn't have good memories of those occasions.

But like so many things with Johann, things were different this time. Despite everything, Frank found himself looking forward to the feel of Johann inside of him.

Right then, Johann gently pushed Frank forward against the railing of the balcony. Turning him around, he took Frank's head in both hands and kissed him, gently, longingly, the tip of his tongue curiously touching along the first line of stubble on Frank's upper lip.

"God, you taste good enough to eat."

"Are you sure you want sex instead of breakfast?" Frank asked with a wide smile.

"I want everything," Johann replied, smacking his lips with a delighted sparkle in his eyes. "Everything of you, with you, and for you."

"How do you manage to make that sound so... not cheesy?"

"Don't know. Honesty, maybe?"

Still smiling widely, Johann took Frank's cock in his hand, gently stroking along the length of it, his thumb caressing the seam of its head, making Frank roll his eyes in delight. Silently chuckling at the effect his touch had on his lover, Johann placed another kiss on Frank's lips, then on his chest, his throat. Working his way further down, he planted small, almost reverential kisses along the way, on his pectorals, his nipples, down along the narrow trail of dark hair that led the way to Frank's cock.

Already suspecting where this would lead, Frank planted his feet wider apart, leaning his back against the railing. Johann, in the meantime, had continued his line of kisses and was now gently licking along the length of Frank's dick. Burying his hands in Johann's hair, Frank watched as his lover swallowed his cock, slowly and thoroughly. It was a wonderful sensation, every time, and with Johann's fingers gently scratching along the taut skin of his balls, Frank knew he would have come almost instantly if they hadn't been at it constantly for the last few days.

But as it was, he could savor the moment, closing his eyes, following each of Johann's moves in his mind, with his hands in Johann's hair. His cock was almost painfully hard now, quivering with anticipation and hot with need.

Finally, Johann let go with a deep sigh; Frank's dick flopping back against his stomach with almost painful hardness.

"I could go on like this forever," Johann remarked dreamily, licking along Frank's cock languidly one more time. "You just taste so good."

"I couldn't," Frank replied, laughing under his breath. "You're getting awfully good at this."

"Really?" Johann looked up, his green eyes sparkling, his lips flushed and shiny and beautiful. "I think I need a lot more training. A lot." Looking back at Frank's dick right before his nose, he added wistfully, "But maybe not today."

Still smiling widely, Johann rose to his feet again, his own dick raising an impressive tent in the pants he still wore. Embracing Frank again, he kissed him, more passionate this time, hungry for sex and definitely not giving the impression of seeing anything wrong in this.

Smiling into their kiss now, Frank let his hands glide down his lover's back, pushing down the waistband of Johann's pants until it slipped over the curve of his ass. With closed eyes, he softly touched the now-exposed skin, allowed his fingertips to run over the fine, downy hair that grew along his crack, chuckling softly as he noticed how his touch made Johann shiver with desire.

Johann apparently didn't want to wait much longer and slipped out of his pants without looking, keeping his lips closely locked with Frank's. When their cocks touched, skin on skin for the first time this morning, he shivered again, groaning almost inaudibly. With his hands, Johann took both dicks together and started stroking them, gently, slowly, his eyes closed, his mouth slightly open. For a moment, they continued like this, their lips so close they were almost kissing, their cocks pressed together and moving ever so slightly against each other.

It was Johann who broke their almost dreamlike state, letting go of their cocks with a husky chuckle.

"Gods, I almost would have made us come."

"What's wrong with that?"

"I want more." Shaking his head, he added, "From you, I always want more. You're like a drug."

Unable to reply anything appropriate, Frank smiled and kissed his lover. Yes, he should doubt every single word Johann said. But seeing him like that, his eyes glazed over with obvious desire that was beyond physical, it was impossible to believe that he was not in love with Frank. Maybe it was a vain thing to hope that they might have a future together after the war. But right now, it seemed like the only thing that mattered.

Right then Frank noticed how Johann had planted his feet wider apart and was about to spit in his hand, as he usually did when he was about to prepare himself. But this time, Frank stopped his lover's hand.

"No." he said softly, smiling at Johann's hungry, confused expression. "The other way 'round, today. I want you to take me."

Silently, Johann blinked in surprise, a soft, startled smile growing on his face.

"Are you sure?" he asked, looking at his lover's face as if searching for clues for this sudden change. "But you said you have never..."

"It's been a long time," Frank lightly adjusted his earlier lie, "and I never really liked it."

Still not entirely the truth, but closer, at least. This really wasn't the moment to spill all those ugly memories. He wanted Johann, inside of him, before the mood left him and he changed his mind.

"You don't have to," Johann said softly.

"I know. But I..." Shrugging at his sudden lack of words, Frank scratched his chest. "I want you. Now."

Taking a deep breath, Johann nodded. It was a wonderful feeling for Frank to see that his lover didn't need many words to understand how important this was, and what a massive step for Frank. They just understood each other without words in moments like these.

"I had been looking forward to you fucking me senseless here on the balcony," Johann finally said. "But we can have that any other day."

Taking Frank by his hand, he led him back inside into the building.

"Come on, let's take this somewhere a little more comfortable and a little less drafty," he said, gently pulling Frank towards the bedroom. "We should take our time, now."

Which was all fine with Frank. It had indeed been a while since he had last been taken by a man, and the thought of Johann preparing him was nice. With a slight smile, Frank realized he didn't feel embarrassed by his lack of experience. He trusted Johann, despite everything.

As Frank had already expected, Johann had opened the window in his bedroom and uncovered the bed before he had come looking for Frank. Now brilliant sunlight was flooding the room, dust motes dancing in the air, the spots where the sunlight hit the wooden floor all warm to their naked feet, adding the scent of beeswax to the lavender of Johann's sheets.

"You want me to close the curtains again?" Johann asked, his body a dark silhouette in the bright light, the sparse fine hair on his body forming a gleaming outline like a halo.

"No," Frank replied, pulling his lover in another, close embrace. "It is perfect."

Johann chuckled softly, gently burying his nose in the small indention just above Frank's collarbone. With his hands, Johann once more wandered down his lover's back, caressing, exploring and memorizing at the same time. On this side of the building, the sun was reaching deep enough into the room to warm them thoroughly, and the chill of the night already was nothing more than a memory.

"Lie down," Johann ordered quietly.

Wordlessly obeying, Frank lay down on his back and watched as his lover picked the small vial of oil from the night stand. Climbing onto the bed with him, Johann knelt down between his legs. While he poured a generous amount of the oil into his hands, he smiled at Frank with an adorable mix of care and excitement.

"You tell me as soon as it feels uncomfortable, yes? We're not in a hurry."

"Well, maybe you aren't," Frank replied, "but damn me if I have to stare at your dick much longer."

His remark sounded light-hearted enough, but inside, Frank was getting more and more nervous. He wanted Johann, he wanted him now. But it still didn't do much to calm his body, to fight the urge to bolt and run that was stirring somewhere deep in the back of his mind.

But then there was the look in Johann's green eyes that reassured Frank that everything would be all right, that he would know when not to press any further.

As if on cue, Johann turned his attention to Frank's cock that was lying exposed in front of him in a bright patch of sunlight that reached through the room onto the bed. With his well-oiled hands, he stroked along the length of Frank's cock, gently, languidly, bringing it to full hardness with the same reverential pacing a musician might show when warming up to a precious instrument.

Taking in a deep breath, Frank relaxed into the pile of starched pillows he had been leaning against, a little surprised at how tense he had been. Taking one of the pillows to his chest, he closed his eyes, completely submitting himself to Johann's caring hands.

If Johann noticed how much of an effort Frank was putting into staying calm, he didn't comment on it. Instead, he continued massaging his lover's cock until the first low moan escaped Frank. Listening to the cues his lover's body gave him, Johann then continued his massage, first along Frank's balls and from there downward towards his ass. Gently, he went on stroking Frank's crack, just a gentle caress with one hand, while the other was still stroking Frank's hard cock.

Silently, they continued this way for a while, just sharing a touch, while Frank had his face buried in a pillow that smelled faintly of Johann.

Then, without a prompt from Johann, Frank pulled up his legs and shifted the tilt of his hips, allowing his lover's hands to go deeper. Gently, almost shyly, Johann continued caressing Frank's crack, his hands warm and slick with oil, until they reached his anus. There, he seemed to pause, and for a moment, Johann returned both his hands to work on Frank's cock. This time, he wasn't subtle in his motions, and stroked his lover until Frank's balls were tingling with urgency. Almost close to his climax, Frank was panting, a thin sheen of sweat glistening on his body.

Frank knew that Johann was just trying to distract him, but it was working nicely. Every time he felt old memories encroaching, the present was always strong enough to hold them at bay. Whether it was the smell of wet sackcloth that reminded him of his miserable first time or the callused dark hands pressing him down onto the concrete floor of the prison in Algiers, it was the here and now that proved much more real.

Again, Johann's hands returned to Frank's ass, and this time, a first finger found its way inside of him. Gently, cautiously, but with a slight insistence that made Frank almost see the naughty smile on Johann's face without opening his eyes. He knew Johann enjoyed this tremendously, the trust, the way he had learned to work Frank's cock to distract him every time without making him come.

Much to his own surprise, Frank felt himself relax rapidly as soon as he felt Johann's finger inside of him. If anything, he suddenly felt hungry, angry at the fact that this all was taking so long. Looking around the pillow he was still cradling to his chest, he growled at Johann.

"What's taking you so long?" he asked, knowing full well that he wasn't exactly fair about this. But then, how else should Johann know that he was now supposed to go a little faster? "You want me to fall asleep here?"

"You think you can take more already?" Johann asked with a naughty smirk, exposing one single canine. "So how about this?"

Carefully, Johann pushed a second finger inside Frank, constantly keeping eyes locked with his lover. Frank found the sensation uncomfortable, but far from actually painful. And he craved Johann's dick inside of him with an urgency that easily overwhelmed any remaining bits of apprehension. Being with Johann would be an antidote to his poisoned memories, like a light to banish the dark shadows of the past. Suddenly, Frank found himself bucking his ass up against Johann's hand, burying the fingers in himself as deeply as possible.

"I'm not fragile. Come on!" Frank all but ordered, surprising himself with how much his voice sounded like the continued growl of a hungry wolf.

Wordlessly, Johann added another finger, his face now reflecting a cautious mix of anticipation and fascination at the sudden enthusiasm of his lover.

This time, Frank found himself almost painfully stretched, but still it seemed only a faint warning against the clamoring of his need. Allowing his head to fall back into the pillows, Frank worked himself on his lover's fingers with a grim determination, pulling tight around him and relaxing again, again and again.

Almost in the same manner he felt himself widen around Johann's fingers, Frank felt his world constrict more and more around his burning desire to feel his lover's cock inside of him, until nothing else around him mattered. With a somewhat jerky motion, he pushed Johann's hands away from him, and instead pulled up the other man to lie on top of him.

The sudden weight and their skins touching made Frank gasp, his mind clearing at least a little. Opening his eyes, he looked into Johann's eyes, wide and green and sparkling.

"Damn, *Süßer*, you surely know how to work up an appetite," Johann said, hardly able to suppress a shiver of desire himself. "You think you're ready?"

"Shut up and fuck me."

Faced with such a clear command, Johann only laughed, kissing Frank with a fervor that spoke of so much affection that it was intoxicating. Gently, he pulled Frank's legs up around his waist, his rock-hard dick touching Frank's ass lightly. Still looking deep into Frank's eyes, Johann took one hand to guide his cock, and cautiously pressed it against Frank's ass. For a moment, Frank wondered if he might be tensing up again, but then he felt the other man glide into him with much less effort than he had expected.

All of a sudden, Johann filled him inside, hot and hard and painfully large, but the pain was nothing compared to the bliss of seeing Johann's eyes widen with pure lust at the sensation.

His mouth working soundlessly, Johann seemed to be searching for words, but Frank just stopped him with another kiss.

No words could do justice to what they were feeling right now. There was a closeness between them, a shared joy and ecstasy that Frank had never encountered before. Moving gently underneath his lover, Frank kept his eyes locked with Johann, their passion rising and ebbing in unexpected synchronicity.

As soon as he was convinced Frank was feeling comfortable, Johann started moving himself. Carefully, at first, with cautious, probing motions, soon enough he was entering Frank with long, languid thrusts, not hard, but strong, deep and passionate. Like waves branding on the shore, he pushed inside Frank again and again with measured movements, wonderful, relentless, filling, fulfilling.

Gasping for air, Frank suddenly realized that this was what people called lovemaking. Not the hard, pleasurable friction that could be so intoxicating in itself. But there was another dimension to the slow build-up in his body and mind this time, in the way he could see his own passion and desire reflected in his lover's eyes, in the way they were linked by more than just their bodies. It was a timeless sensation, floating, his body burning with passion, each new thrust of Johann sending new waves of pleasure through his body. Each time Johann pushed inside of him, they both came a little closer to their climax, each time he pulled out, they managed to catch a breath.

Instead of going faster and faster, as usual when they neared their peak, this time, they were going even slower, savoring each motion, every inch of Johann's dick moving into Frank and out of him again, until they felt like screaming with the intensity of the sensation. Holding each other in a tight, white-knuckled embrace, they finally pushed each other over the threshold simultaneously. Biting and clawing, Johann pumping hot and hard inside his lover, Frank spilling between their sweat-slicked stomachs.

For a long while, neither of them moved, both spent and exhausted and blissfully ignorant of everything else.

Then, with gentle insistence, Frank pushed Johann off him, taking a deep breath when he was finally free of his lover's weight.

His body was still tingling with the aftermath of their lovemaking, the memory of Johann inside of him so vivid and prominent it repeatedly overwhelmed any attempt at getting his wits together again. And Frank couldn't have cared less. Lying here in bed, in a bright patch of warm summer sunlight, one hand on the ass of his lover next to him, life was as perfect as it could possibly be. As long as he didn't think of tomorrow, or anything else beyond their little island in the mist, everything was good.

Pushing himself to a more upright position, Frank smiled at Johann who was still lying as he had fallen off him, a stupid, happy grin plastered all over his face. He looked just as happy as Frank felt.

Grimacing, Frank grabbed a loose corner of the bed sheet and wiped himself clean as much as was possible, the semen on his belly already drying in the sun and sticking to his hair. But it was nothing a cooling bath in the river wouldn't cure, he thought with another smile before he abandoned his task for good.

Giving a deeply satisfied sigh, he reached for a pack of cigarettes from the nightstand. Lighting one, Frank looked out of the window at the tree tops swaying gently in the breeze. The birds had almost stopped singing, a clear sign that it was quite late in the morning by now. Their lovemaking had taken more time than Frank had thought, he realized with a sated smirk.

Groaning something unintelligible but vaguely demanding, Johann suddenly came back to life next to him.

Chuckling, Frank handed him the cigarette, watching as his lover crawled back into a slightly more sitting position as well.

Again, they sat together quietly for a long moment, the cigarette passing back and forth between them. In the end, it was Frank who broke the silence.

"How'd you guess?"

"Guess what?"

"That I am... interested. In you."

Surprised, Johann gave a startled laugh, but there was a note of bitterness in his voice that wasn't lost on Frank when he replied.

"Honestly? I didn't." Smiling fondly at his lover, he added, "Until the moment you asked to see my bedroom, it was nothing but wishful thinking."

"You're crazy," Frank stated, taking the cigarette out of Johann's hand. "Completely crazy."

"Not really." Smiling at Frank's doubtful glance, he explained, "See, I was running out of ideas of how to get the information about my study in the right hands. And if I run out of ideas, that means I am pretty desperate. Then, one night, you come falling out of the sky. That in itself was a coincidence so unbelievable that it bordered on miraculous." Gently, Johann kissed Frank's shoulder before he continued, "And then, after I pulled you out of the mud and into the shed, you turn out to be one of the most beautiful men I have ever seen."

"Oh please, Johann."

"Ah, this is my story, and I can make you as beautiful as I want to." Smiling widely now, he wriggled his eyebrows mischievously. "I can even make you as beautiful as you are."

Defeated, Frank gave up, and instead turned around to better watch Johann tell another of his colorful tales.

"So, when I saw you lying in the shed there, I thought that even God couldn't be that cruel. You were everything I ever asked for — so maybe you could also be the love of my life." Laughing at himself, Johann added, "I still can't believe this is really happening, you and me. But this is real, isn't it?"

"It is," Frank replied firmly, gently nudging Johann with the tip of his nose. "I love you."

"And I love you, too. More than anything else."

Chapter 12
Of Friends and Farewells

September 1946, Nuremberg, Palace of Justice
"Elias, please, you've got to listen."
Frank's urgent plea was almost lost in the constant murmur of the courtroom. But the young lawyer looked up, his pale face betraying the fact that he must have been working through the night again.

"You shouldn't be seen talking to me, Frank." Looking around, Elias seemed to scan the room for potential spies and finding only those. "Today is going to be the only time I know we'll make a point here, so please don't give Jackson any handle to turn things against us again."

"Right, that is what I wanted to talk to you about."

"Oh, no." Elias' face seemed to be void of all color. "What have you done?"

"Nothing. At least, nothing wrong." The doubtful look on Elias' face didn't change one bit, so Frank continued, "I tried to tell you yesterday, after we were in the prison, but you left in such a hurry. I talked to -"

But right then, the rear door to the room was opened with emphasis, and two guards led in von Biehn wearing his gray Wehrmacht uniform. Johann looked still rather worn, but not as bad as he had the first day when Frank had come to Nuremberg. Actually, he looked as if regaining a little color, odd as that was considering the situation he was in.

"I have reserved a seat for you at the rear," Elias pressed out between his teeth. "Go, sit down, maybe we'll have a chance to talk during lunch break."

Frank only nodded. There wouldn't be much point in the lawyer knowing about his talk with Jackson anyway. Either it would make a difference, and Elias would notice soon enough, or it wouldn't. Together with the whole courtroom, Frank rose as another aide announced the judges. All four were present in person today, making clear that they expected to hear and see something worthwhile during today's proceedings.

As unobtrusively as he possibly could, Frank seized the moment to leave the railing he had been standing at to go to the room's rear where Elias had managed to get him one of the exceedingly sought-after seats. About in time with the judges, Frank took his place, next to an elderly man with a white beard streaked with traces of its former dark brown. There was something familiar about that man, Frank realized after a while. So he took some moments to study his neighbor, the other man's simple clothing, the way his eyes looked haunted despite his best attempts not to.

He had seen this man once before, Frank was sure of that. But when?

"Do I know you?" Frank asked softly in German, hoping to have picked the right language.

The other man turned around, with a twinkle in his eyes that answered Frank's question with an obvious yes.

"I remember you, if that was your question," the man replied, smiling widely. "You were in the same truck with me and my family when we all left this country the last time."

Frank's only reaction was a silent "oh" as he remembered the old man in the rear of the truck. There was only a faint resemblance between the emaciated, wild-haired figure in the dark and the soft-spoken man right next to him now, but it was there.

"And just like you," the other man continued, "I am here trying to save a friend."

***

August 1943, Spreewald, von Biehn estate

With a surprisingly familiar creak, the door of the garden-shed opened. That scent of dust and old plants was still there, the faint note of gasoline and paint-stripper that reminded Frank so much of his first days here on this island in the mist.

"Do you remember that I once said all important information was in my head and the Führer's only?" Johann asked, his mirth barely able to conceal how uneasy he felt.

It was their last evening together.

Later, after dinner, von Biehn would lead Frank to a remote meeting point where he would be picked up and brought down south, making for some hardly known trails across the Alps down towards Italy. And from there on, things were sketchily laid out, but much easier anyway. Italy would be dangerous grounds, but nothing a few well-placed bribes wouldn't sort out.

Even though they had made the best out of the days they had spent together, even though they had cherished every second together as much as possible, the thought of farewell was hard on both of them. Too hard, actually, to ignore.

"Of course I do." Frank had made a silent pledge to himself that he wouldn't forget a single word spoken, or a single thing seen during these days. The future looked cloudy at best, and if all things failed, these memories were all Frank would have left to remember of the few days he had been truly and happily in love.

"In this case," Johann explained while rummaging between some white metal chairs, "I was a little bit more literally speaking than maybe expected."

As if in reply to Frank's questioning look, Johann came out of the corner with the gypsum Hitler bust in his hands that had been standing there all the time.

"It is one of the few souvenirs I asked from the University in Tübingen where some parts of my study were assembled," von Biehn explained, his eyes searching the place for something else.

"And what that's got to do with us?"

"Nothing. Everything." Enigmatic as ever, Johann handed Frank the bust only to dive back into the murky depths of the crammed place.

No small wonder he had hidden me here, Frank thought to himself. *He could hide a whole squad among all this junk and no-one would notice.* Not really in the mood to stand around and wait, Frank set down the ugly, staring bust and started folding the crocheted plaid that still was lying where he had left it. Tonight he would leave this place, and by all probability would never return again.

It hurt.

The thought of leaving this place, of leaving Johann's side hurt so much even before it was real that Frank wasn't sure he would be able to stand it for the rest of his life. He felt like a man given a few days in paradise only to be kicked out again, back into his normal, miserable life.

Chicken broth and rye bread. Those had been the first things Frank remembered to have been brought by von Biehn, another memory he wanted to encase in his heart forever. The way the ivy leaves in front of the dirty window were dancing, the croaking of the old oak that overshadowed the shed. Memories, nothing but memories. He was still standing here, but already all he had left were memories.

With a sigh, he put down the plaid and started folding up the recliner to put it back into the same corner as its fellows. But then Johann returned, grinning, a huge sledgehammer in his hands.

"I knew I had seen this blasted thing somewhere," he said, then halted as he saw what Frank had been doing. "You cleaned up."

"Yeah. I thought you liked it tidy. As a German..."

"Sure." Johann sounded so sad Frank felt stupid for his lame attempt at humor. "I just thought... It was the last trace of you being here, *Süßer*. And now there won't be anything left of you once you leave."

"I — I am sorry."

"What for? You are absolutely right." With a sudden gesture, von Biehn grabbed Frank and embraced him, holding him like a drowning man and not showing any sign of ever letting him go again.

"I don't want to go," Frank whispered into their embrace, and he felt Johann nod silently.

"Nor do I want to let you go."

For a moment, both men stood there in silence, the setting sun outside casting a deep orange glow into the small room. Whatever they felt, it didn't change necessities one bit. Neither would Frank stay here, nor would Johann flee with him.

Clinging to each other was pointless, but it still felt so good.

Finally, the two lovers separated again, Johann trying hard for a cheeky smile.

"Here," he said while holding out the hammer to Frank with a gesture towards the bust. "Go hit him hard, and aim for the eyes."

As Frank did nothing but gape wordlessly, Johann added, "You'll see. Come on."

Still doubtful, Frank took the hammer, smashing the bust with a weird feeling of satisfaction, watching the white pieces skitter across the floor.

"See? You didn't get to kill anybody important, but at least you were able to vandalize one of our national symbols," von Biehn commented dryly, kneeling down to sort through the remains.

When he stood up again, he was holding a little black cylinder in his hands, his face serious.

"This is my study, including the final map, on a microfiche archive," Johann explained, handing the little thing over to Frank. "But it is not important. If ever you are in danger of getting caught, destroy it. There'll be copies around the major Wehrmacht offices within a few months anyway, and even your people should be able to obtain one or another of them. But you must survive. You must get back to your people, and tell them I flipped the second and third digit behind the comma of the average concrete strength denominator in the tables for France. They will know what to make of this then."

Once again, Johann sighed deeply, tenderly caressing Frank's cheek with his thumb.

"If for nothing else," he asked softly, his voice so low it was hardly more than a whisper, "will you survive for me?"

"Only if you do as well."

"I promise."

***

September 1946, Nuremberg, Palace of Justice

"Honored Judges," Jackson opened the day's judicial proceedings, "over the last days, prosecution has tried to outline the pivotal role Oberst Johann von Biehn has played in all military and strategic operations of the Third Reich."

Almost everybody in the courtroom nodded in silent agreement with him. Indeed Jackson had done much more than merely outlining his position.

"His defense has tried to make us believe that von Biehn had been nothing but a hard-working son of his country, doing nothing but his job, as extraordinary a job that may seem," Jackson continued. "But what my esteemed colleague has so far failed to mention, is that his charge has also reaped massive profit from the Nazi Regime's ethnic cleansing, and that he has made a personal sport out of other people's suffering."

With a flourish that showed how much Jackson enjoyed the situation, the prosecutor turned back towards his table and patted a stack of black folders he had piled up there.

"This, my Lord Judge, assembled judges, is a compilation of items Oberst von Biehn has been actively searching out in auctions and from private owners during the war. It exclusively contains items that previously were owned by people expropriated by the Nazi Regime." Seeing that neither the judges nor anyone in the audience could see any crime in that, Jackson smiled. There was no doubt that he loved these moments of his profession. "Your Honors, on several occasions Oberst von Biehn has been quoted saying that he was going after heirlooms of enemies of the Reich because it was his 'personal pleasure to collect treasured items of those stupid sods who thought the German people wouldn't act against their treason. Those items remind me of what they have lost and will never regain.'"

Now, a wave of appalled murmurs rolled through the room, and Jackson carefully waited for everyone to calm down before he continued.

"Now does that sound like a man who's oblivious to what happens and merely does his job in the ivory tower of the universities and institutes he worked in? Can a man who tracks down several hundred items of sentimental value to 'enemies of the state' for his explicitly stated personal entertainment be the kind of man the defense is trying to portray here? I strongly doubt so."

Jackson's last words were delivered with all the emphasis of a trained speaker, and their impact lingered in Frank's mind. This information was new to Frank, and he struggled hard to piece this together with the images of Johann he had had so far. It just didn't want to fit.

Frank could see from his place that Elias looked utterly composed, as did Johann on his lonely bench. As disastrous as this new move of Jackson's sounded, it didn't seem to come as a surprise.

Casting a careful look to his side, Frank saw that even the man next to him nodded knowingly, the trace of a smile playing in the corners of his mouth. What was going on here? And why hadn't anybody seen the necessity to inform him? More and more, Frank came to the conclusion that it suited Elias just right that he didn't know about Frank's talk with Jackson.

In front of the judges, Chief prosecutor Jackson returned to his desk and sat down, offering the "stage" to Elias with a well worn-in gesture. Elias in turn rose from his chair, making the whole moment look rehearsed. His voice sounded boyish and inexperienced compared to Jackson's, but that was deceiving, Frank knew.

"Honored Judges," Elias asked though it was clear he was mostly addressing Jackson, "I assume Prosecution has delivered reliable proof of his allegations against my charge."

"Of course," Jackson answered from his chair, not making the effort of standing up. Pointing out how boring he thought the whole question, he elaborated, "Twenty-one written statements under oath, all from witnesses even you will find impeccable."

"Oh, that's neat." Elias' comment was ringing with mirth, and still Frank couldn't believe his ears as he heard the young lawyer saying, "But unfortunately, utterly unnecessary. The defense confirms those quotes as being perfectly correct and truthful."

The ensuing uproar in the audience was deafening.

***

August 1943, Spreewald

The only sound heard in the silence of the forest was the occasional gurgling of the water when Johann dug into the river with the long, iron-shod paddle that came with this kind of boat. The birds that made such a noise from dawn till dusk all seemed to be gone, and Frank wondered if there were any humans around this part of the area except for the two of them.

Sometimes, bright patches of moonlight managed to get through the dense canopy of leaves, glimmering slashes of cool light on silent waters, a night in silver and black. It was a beautiful image, solemn and serene, and quite fitting the occasion. Several times, Frank found himself wondering if being ferried into afterlife would be such a beautiful ride as well.

But it was Johann steering the small barge through the shallow waters, and hopefully it wouldn't be the last voyage Frank embarked upon. Despite better knowledge, Frank hoped that he would return one day, to see his lover again, to see if they would be able to build a mutual future out of what would remain after the war.

Von Biehn, tall and striking as ever, apparently followed similar trails with his thoughts. His face was calm and melancholic, only occasionally did he glance at Frank sitting in front of him.

As expected, they had spent their last day together without losing so much as a word on parting. When Frank had left to pack a small bundle for the voyage, his sniper rifle had been lying on the bed, cleaned and in perfect condition. Just as wordlessly, a revolver had shown up, together with some spare ammunition.

Dinner had passed in mutual silence, as had the following walk and a last drink on the balcony. Somehow, they hadn't even ended up in bed together for a last time, but had been sitting there, cuddled together, holding hands, watching the evening turn into night.

"It's time," Johann had suddenly said, and Frank hadn't been able to do anything else but nod and get up.

So they had gathered up Frank's bundle and some more items Johann apparently had prepared, and left for the island's small pier. There they had boarded a narrow little wedge of a boat, its only engine being Johann and the long, flat-ended stake he used for both propulsion and steering.

Since then, no other word had been spoken between the two men. Even though Frank felt like his chest would explode if he didn't say something soon, everything he could think of seemed banal compared to what he felt. But in the end, the silence was worse than everything else, so finally Frank said, "I don't want to leave you."

In response, Johann smiled softly and nodded. "I know."

"Why don't you come with me?" It suddenly burst out of Frank, even though he already knew the answer. "Just hop on the truck, come with me to Italy, I'll get you a safe passage into the US."

"You know I can't leave," von Biehn replied evenly, though his voice was close to catching. "My country needs me."

Disdainful, Frank gave a soft, bitter laugh. Apparently, it was possible to feel jealous of a whole country.

"I need you too," he said firmly, his own anguish visibly reflected in Johann's face.

"When this war is over, *Süßer*," von Biehn replied, "my whole life will be yours. I promise."

Silently, Frank nodded. He knew this was about as much as he would get, and there was no way he would get more in this silver-sprinkled night.

"I'll take you up on that one," Frank tried to reply lightly, and almost managed.

"I expect you to."

Once again, silence returned to the forest, no sound to be heard except for the occasional soft gurgle of the dark water.

Chapter 13
No Dead Heroes

September 1946, Nuremberg, Palace of Justice

Slowly, the din in the courtroom subsided, leaving Frank with a deep frown on his forehead. What the hell was Elias trying to achieve by agreeing with the prosecution?

"Honored Judges," Elias continued his explanation, "I am rather sure the list my esteemed colleague has presented you with begins with the items formerly owned by a family Rosenthal from Potsdam."

Waiting for a short nod from one of the judges, Elias fetched a form from his desk and handed it over to the court usher, who in turn handed it on.

"Honored High court, I'd like to call Mister Avram Rosenthal as a witness."

"Objection!" Jackson bellowed from his chair. "Unannounced witness."

"Indeed." Lord Judge Lawrence confirmed, looking at Johann's lawyer with curiosity. "Why should we accept this witness?"

"I sincerely have to apologize."

There still was that note of gentle amusement running in Elias' voice, and as the man next to Frank rose, took up his briefcase and started walking down towards the railing that separated the spectators from the actual court, Frank started to guess where this all was leading.

"But until late last night, we didn't know if Mister Rosenthal would make it here, so there wouldn't have been much sense if we'd announced him. Regardless, I still ask you to accept this witness as he'll be able to deliver sufficient proof that he is who he claims to be and will certainly be available for questions from the prosecution. But we think he'll be able to give us some pivotal insights on the issue at hand today."

A questioning glance of Lawrence confirmed that Jackson didn't further object, apparently as he didn't feel it would change the court's ruling. Though, Frank thought he saw a kind of amusement in Jackson's eyes as well, something rather unnerving to the American.

For a moment, the Judges seemed to be discussing whether they'd accept the new witness, then ordered Elias to proceed. The young lawyer helped Mister Rosenthal towards the stall where he would be standing, waiting at his desk while the new witness was sworn in. On his bench, Johann — for the first time since Frank had been here in Nuremberg — indulged in a smile.

"Mister Rosenthal," Elias commenced leisurely, "I am sure my esteemed colleague will spend ample amounts of time to verify your identity, so I allow myself to omit that part."

The new witness only smiled and nodded, apparently well instructed on what was about to happen here in court.

"Just for the records, you are Avram Rosenthal, head of the Rosenthal family of Potsdam, who was expropriated in May 1943 under charges of *Reichsverrat* and then went underground with his family?"

"Yes, I am." Avram's voice seemed frail in comparison with the other speakers, making Frank once again realize how much training there was in Elias' innocuous voice. Had he seemed that small and insecure as well when he had been standing down there, Frank wondered? No surprise Jackson had ripped him to shreds.

"And among your lost possessions, had there been a -" Looking around, Elias seemed to be searching for a paper, one he apparently found on Jackson's desk. Pointing at the prosecutor's much quoted list, he asked, "May I?"

Once again, Jackson indulged him, gesturing to take what he needed. As if it had been his paper all along, Elias took out one of the first pages, reading aloud:

"A pocket watch, eighteen carat gold, with an embossed steam-train on the lid and a dedication inside, reading 'In gratitude, His Majesty Emperor Wilhelm II'?"

"Yes. It was the one given to my grandfather as a gift."

"I've seen that you're wearing a pocket-watch as well today. Did you get a new one?"

"No."

"Now you see me intrigued." Elias seemed to voice the thoughts of everybody in the room. "First you say you've lost that watch, then we read it's been bought by Graf von Biehn for his personal amusement and now you claim it's in your possession again? How?"

"It was in a parcel one day," Avram recounted, "Just the watch, our family's menorah and most importantly, my brother's notebooks and manuscripts."

"So you tell us some nameless benefactor has gathered all those belongings for you and sent them to you? Just like that?"

"Well, there is only one person who'd have known that these things were important to us."

"And who would that be?"

"Graf von Biehn."

Once again, a surprised murmur ran through the court, this time more excited than appalled. Apparently, there were some seriously interesting bits to be heard today. From his seat, Frank could see the various reporters crane their necks to get a better look at the man on the witness stand. Most of them looked as if they were struggling to get awake now that there was something real happening.

"Graf Johann von Biehn," Elias asked his witness, "Oberst of the Wehrmacht?"

"Yes."

"The man sitting over there?"

"Yes." Now a smile of deep gratitude ghosted over Avram's features, and he even managed something like a sketched bow as he nodded towards Johann, greeting him. "My Lord."

Once again, the voices in the background grew louder, this time in wonder at the overly old-fashioned and deferential title. On his bench, von Biehn only nodded, his face polite but otherwise utterly unreadable.

"You have met him before, I assume?" Elias asked, his gestures encouraging Avram to talk freely.

"Yes, on the flight, just after..." Suddenly, the man's voice caught, and he it took him a moment to regain his composure. No one in the courtroom whispered this time, for all had seen their share of tragedies during the war. Remembering was tough, and Avram's efforts were met with honest respect.

"Honored judges," Avram continued with a voice that still sounded suspiciously throaty. "It was when my family was hiding and trying to get out of the country when we first heard of what the Graf was doing."

"With Graf, you mean Graf Oberst von Biehn?" Elias interjected.

"Yes, of course. Though we weren't given a name at that time."

"And what were you told he was doing?"

"Saving people. Getting them out of the country. Protecting them from the Nazi."

"For a fee?"

"Oh no, he wouldn't offer help for money." Avram's reply was ringing with so much genuine disbelief it was hard to think he was making all this up. "No, all that was needed was to convince him we were in need. That we weren't trying to set him up."

"Now doesn't that sound odd? One of the highest-ranking Nazi officers, ferrying people out of the country, people his own government has declared criminals?"

"Oh, he scared the hell out of me when we met, goodness." Shaking his head at the memory, Avram's speech was growing livelier with every sentence. "A meeting was set up by friends so I could talk to the Graf to convince him. All I was expecting to see was a man of my age or even older, any kind of rebel or shadowy figure you might have in mind when life forces you to make such desperate moves. But then the door opened, and all of a sudden I faced a terribly Aryan-looking Wehrmacht officer with all that brass dangling on his chest. By God, I almost died that moment."

Frank could so envision that scene; it was very much like Johann to show up for such an occasion in full regalia. But also, he had probably tried to find out if the people he was dealing with were courageous enough not to break at the first sight of a uniform. And if they were smart enough to trust him despite what he was wearing, sly bastard he was.

"So what happened?" Elias gently nudged his witness to continue.

"Oh, we talked. About my family, about what happened since we had to flee Potsdam, of my brother and my children and my wife and what we hoped to do when we found a safe place to settle down again."

"And then?"

"Nothing. He promised to help us but didn't give any details. We parted, and three weeks later, there was a truck standing next to the old barn we were hiding in to bring us to Italy."

Apparently taking his time to let the story sink in, Elias nodded gravely. "But that still doesn't really answer my question on why he would help you under such a personal risk."

"I... I don't know his personal motives. We never talked about him."

"But you must have formed a personal opinion?"

"Objection!" Jackson's voice was so cutting it made several people in the audience jump. "Witness is led to assumption."

"What is to assume about your own personal opinion? Mister Rosenthal seems to know quite definitely what he thinks."

"Nice try, Mister Blumenstein." Lord Judge Lawrence replied, his face even showing something akin to the traces of a smile at Elias' brazen attempt. "Objection accepted, continue."

"Then let me ask differently: Was there any reason you could see that Oberst von Biehn helped you and your family? What made you so special?"

"Nothing." Giving a shrug, Avram added, "I don't think we were special, he helped a lot of people to get out."

"Did he? How do you know?"

"We weren't alone on that truck, for one, you know that." Now both Elias and Avram smiled, relief showing clearly in their faces. "Also, everybody who was saved with us knew some others the Graf had aided as well. And those knew others, so there was something like a network among those who survived."

"Would they stand witness as well for Graf von Biehn?"

"Oh, of course," Avram confirmed eagerly, "All those I talked to wanted to return a little of the help they had been given. That was what took me so long."

"What took you so long?"

"Well, we're talking quite a lot of people here, many families. I don't think it would be proper for all of them to appear here, so I have allowed myself to bring some letters." Apparently searching for his briefcase the court usher had taken from him, Avram looked around the room.

It took the usher in question several moments to register that his efforts were needed. But after that, he hurried to make sure the briefcase didn't contain anything but papers. Apparently not really satisfied with the results of his rushed search, he decided to keep the briefcase with him and instead only handed Elias a remarkable stack of wildly assorted papers. The lawyer in turn handed them on to Avram, who looked a little embarrassed at the messy look of his documents.

"I really should have put them in a file." he said mostly to himself before he looked up at the judges again. "Honored judges, I have brought letters of more than a hundred families living all across Europe, all of them stating that it is only due to Graf von Biehn's personal intervention they are still alive today."

This time, the usually so expressive audience remained silent with what felt to Frank like genuine speechlessness. *Now this was a show worth coming to court for*, he thought.

"Thank you so much for your efforts, Mister Rosenthal," Elias said calmly as he took the pile of letters from Avram to hand them to one of the judges' aides. "This truly is a help beyond words for our case."

Still, the spectators were silently holding their breath as if expecting another revelation. And they were not disappointed for the young lawyer added in such perfect innocence it almost seemed genuine, "Oh, Mister Rosenthal, I almost forgot."

Rushing back to his desk, Elias took a simple note on a sheet of paper and swiftly signed it, adding the letter to the stack in the aide's hands. "My own testimony was still missing."

Now finally, the spectators started murmuring, like a forest rustling with the first warnings of a mid-August thunderstorm.

"And also," Elias continued, "I think Captain Hawthorne hasn't added his yet."

As he pulled another prepared letter out from his desk and waved it in Frank's direction, the former assassin honestly wished for a hole to disappear in. Suddenly, all the eyes in the courtroom were on him, staring and all asking the same question: What the hell was going on here?

But somehow, Frank managed to get up without seeming too irritated, instead appearing calm and composed as he walked towards Elias with what looked to everybody else like a deliberate pace. Inside his head, though, his thoughts were racing, trying to figure out what Elias was trying to achieve with this rather melodramatic setup.

It made much more impact this way than Frank dryly stating that Johann had saved his life; that much was true. But it also raised the question of why the hell Elias hadn't warned him before, and what exactly was written in that testimony he was supposed to sign. Still being effectively gagged by his own government, Frank didn't really see himself signing anything that would only get them into deeper trouble than the one they already were in.

Coming to a halt at the railing that separated the spectators from the actual court, Frank took the note Elias presented him and like every good citizen, started to read what he was supposed to sign. Behind him, the small crowd in the room was buzzing like a beehive, all of them staring holes into his shoulder blades. But Frank managed to stay focused on the text for long enough to be reasonably sure he wouldn't give away any "classified material" with this testimony. At least, nothing more than what he had already disclosed the first time he had been standing witness.

But Elias had definitely taken care not to write down anything that would infringe this particular problem. Basically, the letter was no more than a written statement that Frank's escape from Germany had significantly been aided by Johann, if not made possible in the very first place. Nothing Frank wouldn't have stated before, so he signed the letter with only a vague question in the back of his mind about whether he was really doing something sensible here. But once again, the soft murmur in the back, intensified and prolonged by the interpreters, reminded him of the fact that in this specific case, looks mattered indeed. After all, it was only Johann's impeccable Nazi past they were fighting.

Without a further comment, Elias took the signed letter from Frank, although he acknowledged with a nod that Frank had so nicely played along.

"Mister Rosenthal," the lawyer continued after he had handed the papers on, "thanks so much for your time, you've been of tremendous help." Turning towards the judges, he concluded, "No further questions, your honor."

"Mister Jackson," Lord Judges Lawrence asked, visibly trying hard to make up his mind about this new information and the way it had been presented, "any questions?"

"Sir, of course, sir." Somewhat hesitantly, the chief prosecutor rose from his chair, his face thoughtful rather than frustrated. "But not right now. Prosecution is asking for recess."

"Couldn't agree more." Even the judges seemed relieved at Jackson's suggestion. "One hour recess!"

***

August 1943, Spreewald

When they arrived at the crossroads, the truck was already waiting.

Frank and Johann had tied the little barge to a small wooden pier that looked just like the hundred others they had seen on their way through the silent forest. Still the moon was shining brightly from the cloudless sky, silver light slanting through the dense roof of the forest.

Since their last conversation, almost an hour had passed, and yet neither of them spoke a word. What was there to say?

The important things were said, and Frank was convinced anything else would trivialize what he felt. After all, screaming and crying really wasn't his style, even though that might have come close to expressing what was going on inside him.

Instead, Frank felt something like relief when suddenly, the narrow path they had been walking on ended on a graveled road, with the huge bulk of a truck taking shape in the darkness ahead of them. Now it was too late for private talk anyway.

As if used to doing so every other night, Johann strode on and knocked against the driver's door. The two men exchanged a few words in German, so low it was hard for Frank to overhear anything. But apparently, all was going as planned.

"Come." Johann said evenly as he returned, leading his lover to the rear of the truck. "We don't have much time."

Not that they ever had much of that anyway.

Together, Frank and Johann opened the flap and Frank found himself stared at by several pale faces in the dark.

"*Alles in Ordnung.*" All is well; Johann calmed the other refugees, introducing Frank, "This man will join you, and help you with getting through to Italy. Listen to him; he probably is one of the best men to have around when you're trying to survive."

"Sure," a young man replied, who looked to be made up from nothing but teeth and ears and an oversize coat. "We're glad for any help given." Reaching out with a narrow hand, the young man said to Frank, "Come on. My name is Elias."

Instinctively taking the offered hand, Frank found himself hauled up onto the truck with a strength that belied Elias' narrow frame. Inside, the moonlight revealed seven more figures, all disheveled and huddled together like people who had seen more nightmares than any person should in their lifetime. *It was typical of Johann to give him another bunch of people to watch out for,* Frank thought. What an odd task to give to an assassin. He would have to reconsider his career choices, though, once he got out of this alive.

"Take care, Frank," Johann said, his voice again sounding as if being close to catching. "And no dead heroes. I need you to return."

"No dead heroes," Frank promised, surprised how even his own voice sounded in comparison. "Take care of yourself. I need someone to return to."

Johann nodded, and by the set of his mouth it was clear that he'd rather not say a word. Instead, he deftly slapped the side of the truck, indicating the driver to start the engine. Suddenly, the vehicle moved on, and through the narrow slit the rear flap left open, Frank could see his lover standing there on a moonlit road, waving, mouthing an inaudible, "*Auf Wiedersehen, Süßer!*"

Luckily, it was then Elias closed the flap, and no one could see the single tear running down Frank's face in the dark.

Chapter 14
Some Things Never Change

September 1946, Nuremberg, Palace of Justice
"Silence!" Lord Judge Lawrence bellowed with a surprising volume for a man of his size. "Silence!"

The recess might have been restful for Jackson and the judges, but for Frank it had been hell.

As soon as everybody important had left the courtroom, Frank had found himself assailed by countless reporters from all over the globe, asking him questions they either should have known by reading the court protocol or weren't cleared to know in the first place.

Unable to find Elias or anybody who'd help him out of this mess without spilling blood, Frank finally had given up and instead resigned himself to answering the harmless questions, ignoring the difficult ones. Which somehow had only seemed to incite the reporters even more, and after more than an hour, when the court finally convened again,

Frank still had been encased in a throng of nosy scribes. Which didn't go well with Lawrence at all, of course.

But in the end, it was the promise of severe punishment and the threat of missing something important when the prosecution got to question the latest witness that convinced the reporters to return to their places in an orderly fashion.

"Now that we have sorted this out, Mister Jackson," Lord Judge Lawrence stated with a certain relief, "would you please continue?"

"Of course." Once again rising from his chair, Chief Prosecutor Jackson looked tired, but there was a malicious gleam to his eyes that made Frank very wary.

"Honored court, this morning has seen new and rather surprising material in this case. I have discussed this case with my team, and they agree that we're in some kind of legal void here. So far, we haven't been able to prove anything apart from von Biehn being an intelligent and diligent man, and now it seems he is a courageous philanthropist as well."

Scratching his chin in a well-placed gesture, Jackson most obviously hesitated before he calmly concluded, "If it is a crime to work as a strategist for your country, we'd have a lot of our own people to sue as well. Therefore, honored court, I am forced to inform you that the prosecution sees no way of continuing this trial any longer without turning this into a mere witch-hunt, which I seriously hope this is not. Prosecution drops all charges and pleads innocent."

For a heartbeat, the whole room sat in deafening silence.

Even the perpetual murmur of the interpreters had come to an abrupt halt as everyone struggled to grasp what Jackson had just said, in complete disregard of court proceedings, Frank probably more than anyone else.

"Well," Elias was the first to comment into the stunned silence, utter disbelief saturating his voice, "I surely won't object to that."

"You can't do that!" Lord Judge Lawrence suddenly burst out, looking as if still searching for the hidden joke. "This is NOT your decision! Jackson, are you out of your mind?"

"No, sir, I am not. And, sir, with all due respect, I just did." Looking as if he hadn't done anything out of the ordinary, Jackson earnestly started packing up the files on his desk, apparently considering the matter settled for good.

"I — I," the elderly judge stammered, looking for help from his colleagues who were just as speechless as Lawrence himself. "Jackson, at my desk," he ordered sharply. "Now."

But the trial's chief prosecutor only looked up, giving the assembled judges a hard stare that made Lawrence blink.

"Are you sure?" he asked coldly, with a caustic aggression to his words that felt outrageous to a man of reason like Jackson. "Are you really sure you want to hear my opinion?"

Somehow, the tone of Jackson's question kicked Frank's mind into gear again. He remembered that tone. He had heard it before, the night he had sneaked into the prosecutor's bedroom. Only then it had sounded a lot less... consequential. But that impression now seemed to have been rather deceiving.

"At my desk." Lord Judge Lawrence didn't seem impressed with Jackson's anger, only angered himself.

But that was about the last concern on Frank's mind right then. Together with the other spectators, he slowly realized that if Jackson seriously managed to uphold his bold move, Johann might be free. Blinking rapidly, Frank tried to come to terms with this sudden resolve. Deciding upon guilt or innocence of a man on trial was the part of the judges, not of the prosecutor. However, Jackson wasn't an idiot.

The prosecutor was standing at the judges' desk, arguing with his usual fervor, though he was speaking too softly to be overheard where Frank was sitting. Especially as one by one, the other spectators came back to their senses and seemed to start babbling all at once. Within a few moments, the whole place was in an uproar, and for once, Lord Judge Lawrence didn't even seem to notice.

Frank looked over to Johann on his lone bench and found his lover sitting there, looking composed and smiling; right at him. As if all this had been Frank's doing.

Well, maybe in a way it was.

Right then, the Russian judge took the gavel and decided that there was no need to prolong this chaos any longer. With a few clipped words, he put the trial on recess for an unspecified time, announcing that he and the other judges together would gather to hear a full report on Jackson's absurd maneuver and to decide on the further proceedings.

Then the whole room seemed to explode as suddenly, all reporters jumped from their chairs to be the first to get to one of the few telephones. Only Frank remained seated, a tiny smile creeping into the corner of his mouth, as he realized for the first time in what seemed like years to him, there actually was hope.

***

September 1946, Bedroom of Chief Prosecutor Jackson

"And what do you think to gain by breaking into my bedroom and telling me your heartbreaking but otherwise utterly unfounded story?" Jackson asked sternly, his voice hardly as soft as Frank had asked him to speak.

"Honestly?" Frank asked with a rather cheeky smile. "I am not sure."

Jackson had, much to Frank's expectations, reacted mostly unexcited about his sudden appearance about an hour after the prosecutor had gone to bed. He had, though, threatened to call the guards if his surprise visitor didn't come up with a truly convincing reason for all this.

And so far it seemed the whole story of Frank's capture by Johann and their developing friendship, of the study that finally led to the choice of the Normandy beaches as anchorhead for the re-conquest of central Europe had been sufficiently interesting, if not exactly convincing.

Sitting at the foot of Jackson's bed while the prosecutor sat upright against his pillow, Frank found the whole scene weirdly unspectacular. Somehow, his whole life seemed to become more and more a string of things done differently than normal. Whether his latest bold move would turn out to be a help or hindrance remained to be seen.

"I had hoped that this story might shed some light on why our government so adamantly refuses to let me tell my story."

Now Jackson, who had so far listened with close to no visible reaction, nodded in comprehension. The only light in the little room was what came in from the city night, and Jackson seemed frail and tired in the pale light, his dark hair thinner and his jowls more pronounced. And still Frank could almost see the thoughts racing behind his eyes.

"It makes sense, in a most unpleasant way." Jackson stated mostly to himself. "But once again, why in the world should I believe a word of what you said?"

"Why in the world shouldn't you?" Frank shrugged, hoping he had judged Jackson correctly. "Why in the world should I risk all this, risk my job and reputation at home, risk my life and the whole trial I am here for by coming to you?"

"Well, I could think of several reasons," Jackson replied coldly, professionalism ringing in his voice. "Most of them rather unpleasant." Obviously tired, Jackson stretched and stifled a yawn, only to return his calculating gaze back to the man sitting on his bed.

"But apart from what I believe or not — if there was any credibility to your story, and I was inclined to agree to your justified complaints about how this trial is handled by the Allied government — what would you expect me to do?"

"Set Johann free. He's innocent."

Softly, Jackson chuckled, and there was not even an ounce of mirth in the sound. "That is not my job, boy. Even if I wanted to, the decision belongs to the judges, and them alone."

"Probably." Frank was rather sure the other man was testing him and his determination. But that was one of the few things Frank had plenty of. "But a man as experienced as you are surely has his ways. And even if not, you'll think of something."

This time, Jackson's snarky chuckle was genuine. "Probably, yes."

Silence spread in the tiny room, only broken every now and then by the laughter of Jackson's guards down the hall.

"Actually," Jackson said after quite a while of thinking, "I have come to the conclusion that my security is a little below optimal."

Smiling, Frank nodded. It hadn't been easy to get onto the roof and through the window, even with his extensive experience. But it had not been as hard as it should have.

"I expect a written report from you tomorrow morning suggesting some improvements." There was no questioning Jackson's words, it was a clear order. But an order Frank didn't really mind. "I am sure you have your ways of getting the paper onto my desk discreetly."

Again, Frank nodded. This man was a swift thinker and not shy of using the resources he had. Not necessarily a nice guy, but perfectly qualified for his job.

"And now I would ask you to leave," the prosecutor concluded, "as it's been a long day. Significantly longer than expected."

"Goodnight, then." Frank tipped his imaginary hat and rose to climb through the window he had used to sneak into the room. But Jackson's voice stopped him.

"Captain Hawthorne?" As Frank halted, already halfway out on the window-sill, Jackson said, "Whatever I am going to say in court, I would like you to know that I respect your courage. Our whole judicial system is based on the determination and fixation of the truth. And I resent the idea of someone meddling with that."

Now what was that supposed to mean, Frank wondered? There was a subtle, roiling anger in Jackson's voice, but if it was directed against the government for the non-disclosure order or against Frank for his nightly visit, the reason wasn't easy to make out. And apparently, Jackson wasn't inclined to explain.

"Would you please close the window behind you, Captain Hawthorne?" Jackson asked, rather politely hinting that he considered their conversation over.

"Of course."

Slipping out onto the narrow ledge that ran around the outer walls, Frank closed the window without a sound. Slowly, he climbed up towards the roof to disappear into the night again, all the time wondering if his visit here tonight had been helpful to Johann or if he had just sealed their fates.

***

November 1946, Nuremberg

It was a November morning as cold and bright as they could come. The sky was cloudless and glaring in the palest blue, a soft breeze carrying with it a faint glitter of frost.

On the square in front of the prison in Nuremberg, merely a few steps down the street from where the trials had been held, Frank waited next to a lamppost. His breath left feathery clouds in the air, and he felt the cold sting on his cheekbones. But the calm beauty of the morning and the almost crystalline air were completely lost on him.

Frank's eyes were fixed on the prison's gray metal door, his stance restless and excited. Today, Johann would be released.

That was, Frank immediately dampened his hopes, if everything went as he had been told yesterday.

And he had been told quite a lot over the last two months. Since the moment Jackson had officially dropped his charges against Johann, even though it had never been in his competences, the whole trial had been a mess. Jackson's statement had been revoked, returned, declared a misunderstanding and what not. Frank still felt dizzy from the whole thing. But behind the scenes, Elias and Jackson had, though never officially, been pulling strings, and quite well apparently. At least that was what Benny had told him during their occasional pub nights.

Tons of very high-profile correspondence had crisscrossed the place, sometimes even lagging down the other trials. In the end, Jackson had remained chief prosecutor despite several attempts to change it, but in turn finally revoked his statement. The other trials had come to an end a month ago already, but still Johann's case remained unresolved. Then, out of the blue, the judges had declared they had reached an understanding and were ready to read the verdict. Which had been done last afternoon, and despite everything, Johann had been found guilty.

Still smiling at the shock that Lord Judge Lawrence's words had created, Frank shook his head. Indeed, Johann had been declared guilty. But guilty of nothing more than fraud, embezzlement and obstruction on several accounts. The verdict also stated that all his properties which had been confiscated were kept to compensate the state for its losses, and that the amount of time Johann had spent in jail already was to be deducted from the whole punishment.

Which meant he would be released this very morning.

Shaking his head, Frank wondered if the verdict was the judicial interpretation of a political stalemate. Or a mere joke. But it seemed as if all sides had gotten what they wanted this way.

Right then, a person in a rust-colored coat stepped through the prison gate, and Frank had to blink several times before he believed what he saw.

There was Johann, his dark blond hair neatly parted, looking smart and dashing as if the gray-faced, shy prisoner had never existed. Setting down the suitcase he had been carrying, Johann stretched, in no hurry at all. He had not yet seen the man on the other side of the place waiting for him, instead he calmly started to light a cigarette.

Still Frank had a hard time believing it. As if the last years of the war and the time since then had never passed, suddenly the man he had fallen in love with was back again, after what felt to Frank like several lifetimes. Not that he minded, not at all. But it was so hard not to think he was dreaming.

Taking a deep breath, Frank stepped away from the lamppost he had been waiting at and walked across to the man he had risked so much for. Despite his urge to run and tightly hug his lover, Frank managed a decent walk, looking like the average friend picking up someone from prison.

It took Johann only another second to notice Frank, and still not showing any hurry himself, he picked up his suitcase again and walked closer to meet him. They reached each other about halfway, two lone men on an empty square one very cold November morning.

"Hey," Frank said after he realized that someone would have to say something and stretched out his hand, "Good to see you."

Johann raised a questioning eyebrow but didn't comment. Instead, he took the offered hand and used it to pull Frank into a tight embrace, holding him. "*Hallo, Süßer,*" he whispered.

Holding Johann in his arms again, Frank suddenly realized how much the insecurity of the last weeks had weighed him down. Now it was as if a lump of lead had been taken from his heart, and he could breathe freely for the first time. Slowly, Frank noticed that under the fashionable coat, Johann felt much bonier than he actually should, and that the other man leaned against him as much for support as for comfort.

"Is everything alright?" Frank asked, taking a step back to have a clear look at Johann's face.

"I'm fine. I'm only tired, and hungry. Nothing that won't heal with a little time and care."

The last words were delivered with such a delicious indecent undertone that Frank's worries were immediately dispersed. Whatever the looks, Johann was still very much his impossible self.

"I missed you," Frank said, struggling hard not to kiss the other man out here in a public place. "Very much."

Johann smiled and nodded.

"That scar on your face is new," he remarked, only in the very last moment keeping himself from touching Frank's cheekbone. "It suits you. But I hope it's the only new one."

"Only this one."

It was obvious that Frank didn't want to talk about how he got the scar, and Johann didn't press any further. At least, not directly right now.

"You saved my life," he said instead. "I think we're on even terms, now."

"Elias saved your life. I had very little to do with the whole thing."

"Now didn't you?" Johann asked, taking a long pull of his cigarette. "Robert was telling me something rather different there."

"Who?"

"Robert Jackson. You met him at court."

Surprised, Frank opened his mouth. Then he realized that he was about to say something rather silly and shut it again. What had he expected? Johann wasn't quite out of prison yet, and already spinning webs. It was good to see that some things truly never changed.

"So, what now?" Johann asked, blinking at the harsh winter sun, once again being a little swifter than Frank in his plans.

"I have a room we can share." Frank replied, already knowing that this hadn't been what Johann had asked for. "I don't know," he admitted, "I have never thought beyond this moment."

Looking at Johann's smiling face, Frank knew this was exactly what Johann had expected.

"You could come with me, this time," Frank offered half-heartedly, not really in the mood to discuss their mutual future now and here and in the middle of a freezing square right in front of the prison. "I could find a job, and we could-"

But Johann shook his head.

"I can't leave now," he explained gravely. "I know I promised you otherwise, and if you ask me to, I will go wherever you want. But as long as you haven't made any real plans, I suggest we stay in Europe."

Not really happy about this but also not really surprised, Frank crossed his arms in front of his chest.

"But what's left for you here?" he asked, a little petulant. "Your fortune is gone, and most of your connections as well. Wouldn't it be better to start someplace new?"

"My country is still here." The way Johann pronounced it made clear that country to him was much more the actual soil and people rather than any political body. "Berlin and Hamburg and Dresden and Kassel and so many other cities are no more than rubble. The whole country is occupied, the whole continent torn by war. There is a lot of work to be done. A lot of rebuilding. And I would be glad if you allowed me to be part of that."

Sighing, Frank nodded. There was nothing he wouldn't allow Johann, as long as they did it together. And it wasn't as if he had much of a life to return to in the US.

"So what do you suggest, then?" Frank asked. "As you've had some time on your hands lately, you surely have made better plans than I have?"

"I sure did." Tongue-in-cheek, Johann picked up his suitcase and started walking, apparently quite well knowing where to. And to Frank it very much looked like the direction of the train station. "Do you have enough money for a train ticket to Lake Como?"

"Where?"

"*Il lago di Como*, Lake Como. A lovely lake in the Alps, in Switzerland or Italy or whatever country it is these days. France, maybe?"

"You're not seriously suggesting we go on vacation now?"

"Well, why not?" Johann looked straight at his lover, his eyes sparkling with so much boyish glee that Frank once again was hard-pressed not to kiss him right there. "I have an aunt there who'd love to have us over for some time."

"An aunt?"

"Well, not really an aunt, but a lovely elderly lady remotely related to me."

Wriggling his eyebrows at Frank, Johann explained conspiringly. "She took care of some stuff of mine that I'd like to recollect." As he still saw no understanding in Frank's face, Johann added, "Like most of my money."

"You didn't!" It burst out of Frank, as he began laughing with bewilderment. There it was again, this exhilarating, dazzling and endlessly irritating feeling of always being a step behind.

But Johann only smiled and wriggled his eyebrows again.

"Love you," he replied under his breath, only to have Frank nod in agreement.

"You'd better."

Laughing, Johann went on walking down the road, Frank at his side.

So it would be Frau Haselönner's Bed & Breakfast first to pick up his stuff, then Lake Como, and then wherever Johann's weird plans would lead them.

And that was about the best possible future Frank could think of.

Chapter 15
Epilogue - Bellagio

Christmas 1946, a villa near Bellagio, Lake Como
"There was a parcel for you in the mail today," Frank remarked as he thumbed through the pile of correspondence that was waiting near their morning coffee. "From Paris.... Goodness, Johann, have you told *everyone* where we are staying?"

Laughing, Johann shook his head. "Only my closest and most trustworthy friends."

Still chuckling, he continued checking the fire in the ornate cast iron oven in the corner of the room. Apparently satisfied, he merely dropped another log inside and closed the lid again, while Frank continued pouring their morning coffee.

The last weeks had been blissfully uneventful.

They had left Nuremberg for Lake Como the day Johann had been released from prison. And even though traveling through Europe was still far from easy, they had managed to arrive at the villa of Johann's 'aunt' mere three days later.

Unsurprisingly, they had found that their special talents complemented each other nicely. While Johann seemed to be able to circumvent every kind of red tape that the new governments were putting in their way with a smile and a few remarks, he definitely was out of his depths when the needed infrastructure just wasn't there. But then, working around things being different than expected was what Frank had been living with for the last years of his life. So if the train had broken down for good, he found them a bus. Or a ride on a donkey cart to the next bigger town. Or a lift with a family visiting their far away friends for a wedding, who shared their already crammed car and sparse food with a hospitality that made it almost seem as if there hadn't been a war at all.

When they finally arrived in Bellagio in the dead of the night, both Frank and Johann had been wondering how they had managed to survive so far without each other.

Waking the household of Johann's aunt, on the other hand, had seemed an insurmountable obstacle in comparison. But once everyone was up and about, both men had been welcomed like long lost sons. They had been given adjacent rooms in the sprawling lakefront *palazzo* Aunt Lucilla occupied all by herself with her servants; and if she suspected anything about the special relationship between her guests, she never even so much as batted an eyelash.

Since then, their days had been uniformly peaceful and restorative.

Apart from a few dinners and an occasional excursion to the city, Auntie Lucilla kept mostly to herself. She had developed a slight, grandmotherly crush on Frank, though, and remarked on several occasions that she regretted not being a few dozen years younger. So maybe her crush wasn't that grandmotherly, after all.

During the rare moments they hadn't been busy 'getting to know each other again', Johann had been catching up on the news and politics of the new Europe, which consisted of reading piles of newspapers, writing correspondence and talking on the phone for hours. At least, it felt like hours to Frank, who had to admit that he was a little jealous of everything that Johann was spending his time with that was not him.

The whole situation was still feeling absurd, anyway.

There he was now, together with the love of his life, in a beautiful manor at one of the most beautiful lakes in Europe. The war was over, and the future was just waiting for them. From what Frank had gathered, Johann had managed to squirrel away significant funds before he had been captured. Vastly significant funds. Neither of them would ever have to work another day in their lives.

But in a way, that prospect was scarier to Frank than the war had been. They would have to figure out some kind of arrangement where he wouldn't feel like Johann's personal assistant, always trailing behind where he led him across the globe. Not that he minded to be a quiet presence next to exuberantly extrovert Johann, but he was also aware that this would not be a long-term solution.

Though right now, long-term solutions could wait just a little longer.

Like every morning, Johann had slept in, while Frank had gone on a brisk walk along the shore. And even though the weather here at the lake was extraordinarily mild, it still showed that it was late December. It was cold outside, the wind biting through his clothes. So when Frank had returned, he was happy to see that Johann was already up.

Also like every morning, the servants had prepared a small breakfast for them in the usual room. Coffee and croissants, jam and some cheeses, newspapers and, of course, their correspondence. It had taken only a few days for the first letters for Johann to arrive, and their numbers had only been growing since.

But the large, slightly battered-looking parcel that had arrived this morning was the first of its kind.

"Anyone sending you Christmas presents?" Frank asked as Johann picked up the paper-wrapped packet from the sideboard where it had been waiting.

"No idea," Johann replied, yet smiling as if he already suspected something. "But there's only very few people in France who know where I currently am, so that leaves only a tiny circle of suspects."

Sitting down next to Frank, Johann opened the parcel, carefully picking out a folded letter and leaving the rest of it undisturbed. As soon as he had scanned the tightly written page, a wide smile grew on his face, his eyes sparkling like they did so often lately.

"It is a Christmas present, indeed," he said, his beaming expression fading into a warm, fond smile. "From a very dear friend who I met while she worked for the *Résistance*. And it is for the both of us."

"You told your friend in the *Résistance* about 'us'?"

Still smiling, Johann lowered the letter, looking at Frank with stars in his eyes.

"When we met in Paris, I told her I met a 'special someone', and that this special someone was an *américain*. And that I was very, very much in love. No more."

"And now she is sending us a Christmas present?"

Johann only replied with a shrug and an enigmatic smile, then returned to reading the letter. Frank's curiosity got the better of him and he started rummaging through the parcel. Hidden underneath a pile of crunched-up newspaper, he found a suspiciously flat and square gift, wrapped with a lot of love and little handiness in a piece of old wallpaper and a red bow, the latter pressed flat by the hardships of the travel.

"Oh this is adorable," Johann suddenly remarked. Looking up at Frank, he explained, "Here, I've got to read this to you."

Leaning back in his chair, Johann took a sip of his coffee first. Then, he took up the letter again, reading out aloud.

"*Mon cher Jo'ann*," he started, pronouncing his name so oddly it sounded as if he was impersonating that French friend of his, writing the letter. "Please, find enclosed a little gift of mine. I think it will make you and your 'special someone' happy. It sure has brought a lot of joy to my life."

Slightly amused, Frank eyed the still wrapped gift in his hands. A lot of joy? To him, it looked like an ordinary music record, a single at that. But with Johann's friends, one should be careful, things were often much more than they seemed.

"Maybe you do not remember the words you have used to describe the happiness you have found in the arms of a certain someone, but those words have stuck with me." Johann continued reading, gesturing at Frank to open the gift already. "As my life revolves around songs, I turned them into lyrics, the first time I have written anything. Of course, *Louiguy* and the others considered it *de la merde*, and I have kept it in the drawer for almost two years."

By now, Frank had finished unwrapping their gift, and as expected, it was a music record, apparently fresh out of the press and still smelling faintly of solvents.

"But last spring, I insisted on playing the *chanson* live in concert, and it has become one of my most popular numbers. Attached, you will find one of the first prints of my latest single, which will be on the shelves within a few months. There are moments in my life when I understand what you said to me that day when we met, and I hope the two of you will find the happiness you deserve." Taking a deep breath that almost sounded like a sigh, Johann concluded, "*Bises, Édith.*"

Looking at the brightly colored sleeve of the single, Frank connected the pieces of the puzzle Johann was presenting him.

"You know Edith Piaf?" he asked, slightly incredulous even though he knew he shouldn't really be surprised.

"Well, of course," was Johann's tongue-in-cheek reply. "Who doesn't these days?"

"Personally, I mean. I bet she doesn't send dedicated singles to all of her fans."

Johann just rolled his eyes, emptied his cup of coffee and stood up, taking Frank by his hand.

"Come on," he said, "we've got to find a record player. I think I have seen one downstairs."

Not really in the mood to press the matter any further, Frank allowed his lover to lead him back to the ground floor, into the library where Auntie Lucilla had placed this year's Christmas tree. It was a beautiful room, large French windows opening to the lakefront, currently allowing in the cool light of a late December morning.

Unlike the von Biehn manor, this villa already had electricity installed in every room, and accordingly the record player was a recent model. Apparently, Auntie Lucilla was one of the rare elderly Ladies who didn't shy away from new technologies at all.

Soon, Johann had the player set up on a tea table next to the Christmas tree. Frank handed him the single, eyeing the sleeve with a mix of fascination and dread.

"*La Vie en Rose*?" he asked. "Life in Pink? What on earth did you tell her?"

"I don't remember exactly," Johann replied softly, stepping back from the record player as the first notes started to peal out of its speakers. "But I am sure we will find out soon enough."

Gently, almost shyly, the song started.

On the melody of a slow waltz, Edith recounted her love for a man, her love, her joy, the beating of her heart each time she saw him. It was just a simple chanson, and her voice wasn't classically beautiful. But her voice carried the emotions of a lifetime with breathtaking force, and it made the plain melody all the stronger for it.

As both understood the French lyrics quite well, they listened intently and in silence, until Johann sneaked a hand into Frank's, squeezing it gently. Chuckling softly, Johann pulled his lover into a close embrace, his feet moving in step with the melody, almost dancing.

"Now I remember," he whispered into Frank's ear. "I said to her, with him around, I can't be a cynic. When he pulls me into his arms, when he talks to me so softly, it's as if I see the world through rose tinted glasses."

"Oh god, Johann, please tell me you didn't," Frank replied just as softly, feeling embarrassed even though it was a secret just between the three of them. And he didn't even know her.

"I did," Johann insisted, though. "And I meant every single word of it. *Dans tes bras, je vois la vie en rose.*"

With a soft sigh, Frank let his head drop against his lover's shoulder. "You're the least cynical person I know."

"Well, that's only true when you're around." Johann replied with a chuckle.

Not really in the mood to argue, Frank only mumbled something unintelligible against Johann's chest. *How could it feel so good just to be around him?*

They were still embracing when the song ran out, and when the player started from the beginning, Johann's feet started moving again. With gentle insistence, he pushed Frank to follow suit, and soon they were dancing slowly, entwined, cheek to cheek, the whole world around them forgotten. It was a wonderful feeling, just him and his love, dancing a slow waltz, the music around them speaking directly to their hearts.

Though of course, it couldn't last.

"Please Johann," Frank suddenly said as he realized what they were doing, quite abruptly disentangling himself from their embrace. "What if the servants see us?"

"They will think us perverts, scoff, and continue not to notice anything, just as before."

Johann's reply was meant to be lighthearted, but it was obvious how much the secrecy around their love pained him. For a moment, he seemed to wonder what to do, then tried to busy himself with the record player, but finally it broke out of him.

"I am sick and tired of hiding!" he exclaimed with passion. "We're not doing anything wrong, we don't hurt anybody! Why is it *us* who have to hide?!"

"Johann, you know why." Frank could understand his lover's rage all too well, but there was no arguing with the way things were. "We're not normal. We are freaks."

"Maybe we are different. But we are not *wrong*." Taking a deep breath and a few pacing steps, Johann tried to calm himself down again. "Or do you think there is anything wrong about what we feel?"

"No." The answer was out faster than Frank could think. But even thinking about it didn't change what he felt. "There is nothing wrong with what I feel for you. But the rest of the world thinks different."

"*Der Rest der Welt kann mich mal am Arsch lecken!*" Johann bellowed in German, so loud it made the chandelier above them ring. But with his anger vented, his outrage slowly seemed to be turning into grim determination. "I don't care. Let them foam with outrage, but I don't care."

Still, Johann was fixing his lover with that determined look that told Frank he was planning something. For a moment, they just looked at each other, Johann's chest still heaving.

Then, he apparently made a decision that instantly seemed to lift his mood.

"I have postponed this way too long. And I'd be such an idiot to wait any longer," Johann said, his eyes suddenly gleaming. "Stay right where you are, I'll be back in a heartbeat."

Before Frank could even think about asking what his mercurial lover was up to this time, Johann was out of the library and running up the staircase to their rooms. Only a few moments later, he could already hear Johann returning, taking several steps at once, rushing like a little boy late for dinner.

Flushed but beaming widely, Johann returned to the library, his hair that was usually so very neat in adorable disarray. He looked wonderful, Frank suddenly realized. Wonderful and brilliant and alive and just a little bit crazy. By God, he loved this man so very much. How could any of this be wrong?

"Frank," Johann said firmly, the seriousness of his tone in stunning contrast with the sparkle in his eyes. "You know I love you, and that I would do anything for you. But I do not think I have stated my intentions with sufficient clarity so far."

For a heartbeat, Frank wondered what the hell his lover was trying to tell him.

But then Johann in all earnestness went down on one knee in front of him, his hands holding the ring he had fetched from his room. Instantly, Frank's confusion was replaced by slightly horrified anticipation and an unexpected, nose-tingling giddiness.

"I do not know when there will be a day when we two will be allowed to marry. Or even if there will be," Johann continued. "But, I want you to know that you would be the one. I would be honored to spend the rest of my life at your side, and I would be honored beyond words if you would accept my proposal. Captain Frank Hawthorne, would you marry me?"

For a long, long moment, Frank's mind felt empty. Had Johann seriously just proposed to him?

Of course, it would never be, it was a travesty, a perversion of what the whole world around them believed. But this wasn't about the whole world. This was about them. About their lives. About their love.

And there was no doubt about that.

"Yes." Frank answered firmly, surprised how close his own voice sounded to catching. "Yes, I would marry you. Any of these days."

Stifling an embarrassed chuckle, Frank watched as Johann took his hand and gently slid the ring onto his left ring finger.

"This was my father's signet ring," Johann explained. "I guess he would roll over in his grave if he knew what I was using it for. I just think it suits you perfectly."

"Thank you."

Frank was still too stunned for proper words that matched the enormity of his feelings. But then he realized Johann was still kneeling in front of him, and gently pulled his lover off the floor.

"Before anyone sees us," he said gently, hoping not to incite another rage in Johann.

But Johann only smiled.

"Fuck them, I say." Taking Frank's head into both his hands, he kissed the other man on the mouth, passionately and in absolutely no way discreetly. "You are the best thing that has happened to me in all my life, and I will be damned if I ever feel ashamed for loving you."

Blinking, Frank could only nod. This was pretty much exactly how he felt about his love for Johann as well, and there was very little he would add to that.

Except maybe one thing.

"Then kiss me again, you crazy bastard!"

The End

We hope you enjoyed your time with Frank & Johann.

For more information about our books, visit us at www.Brackhaus.com